Alecia's home is in the city of Minneapolis but why is her heart being pulled to the ranches and open fields of Oklahoma?

Later, alone in her room, Alecia once again thought about her confrontation with Rayne that afternoon. If only she had used wisdom and patience. Why was she so overly concerned about a child she might never see again after two months? Perhaps it was an outgrowth of the restlessness she was experiencing at having to stay here.

Thoughtfully, she sat on the edge of the bed brushing her hair. She wanted to have a peaceable spirit. She wanted to be able to look at the people and circumstances through the eyes of patient love. And yet she had been guilty of letting her emotions rule. She wanted to apologize to Rayne and begin again. But how? She was sure he had given her no more thought than he would to a pesky horsefly.

"Give it up," she scolded herself as she changed into her gown and slipped between the cool sheets. "Teach the children at Charlesy School, finish the term quietly, and get back to Minneapolis where you belong."

She fell asleep by turning her thoughts to Galen Rustin, their work together, and his dependable tenderness toward her.

NORMA JEAN LUTZ began her professional writing career in 1977 when she enrolled in a writing correspondence course. Since then, she has had over 200 short stories and articles published in both secular and Christian publications. She is also author of five published teen novels.

Fields of
Sweet Content

Norma Jean Lutz

Heartsong Presents

In memory of Hilda Stahl:
Fellow Author
Sister in the Lord
Encourager
Friend
Her legacy lives on.

ISBN 1-55748-425-2

FIELDS OF SWEET CONTENT

The time-worn hardwood floor came alive with creaks and moans as Alecia Winland moved toward the tall windows of the rural stone schoolhouse. Mellow beams of morning sun intensified the bronze highlights of her thick chestnut hair. Moodily, she lifted her hair off her neck and gazed out at the playground where the laughter and shrieks of the students floated back to her on alfalfa-scented breezes.

Beyond the school yard, on the silver ribbon of highway that split the spring green pastureland, a local farmer was perched on his slow-chugging John Deere tractor. The tractor was in turn slowing the frustrated driver of a semitrailer rig impatiently locked in behind him.

Alecia identified with the rig driver's being forced to slow down to the tractor's pace. This rural Oklahoma ranch land had compelled her to slow her pace as well and like the trucker, she was searching for a quick escape.

A sigh slipped through her unsmiling lips as the rig, glinting in the sun, found its break and surged ahead to freedom, sending excited puffs of black exhaust against the cloudless sky. Regretfully, Alecia was still locked in.

"For I have learned," she had read in Chapter Four of Philippians just this morning, "in whatsoever state I am, therewith to be content." Why then was she chafing at having to be here? Silently, she prayed for the verse to be fulfilled in her life during these days.

Shading her eyes against the morning sun, she watched the children riding the swings as high as they would go. In the inner city school where she had taught in Minneapolis, the swings weren't so high, and the children were never allowed to "pump" one another. Here at Charlesy School, five miles from the nearest town, situated on the edges of nowhere, the children were allowed to soar in keeping with the free creatures they were bred to be, on this wind-swept land.

In her own childhood days, spent in a relatively small Nebraska town, quiet games such as ball and jacks or sidewalk skating were her pastimes. And never with boys. Her older sister, Nancy, and her mother had strictly warned her about the dangers of becoming a tomboy. Quite different from these children out on the playground.

Lyle Jenkins, the multipurpose principal, teacher, and bus driver had playground duty that morning. For that, Alecia was grateful. She disliked the job because she couldn't bear to watch the children swing so dangerously high.

The paunchy, graying Mr. Jenkins was hunched over, carefully explaining the handholds on the baseball bat to a chubby third-grader. This man who was infinitely patient and easygoing with the children was a marvel to Alecia who had observed the gamut of educators from the best to the worst.

Suddenly, her attention shifted as a late model, royal blue pickup turned into the gravel drive at the front of the school. J.D., the curly haired student who hopped out, could easily have been mistaken for a boy had Alecia not known otherwise. Curious, Alecia stepped nearer the window, reaching up to hold the shade cords and entwining them around her fingers as she craned to see. On the door of the pickup were the white words, EL CROSSE RANCH. Below that was a scrolled L with a tiny cross in the bottom loop.

Alecia barely caught a glimpse of the driver before he backed out of the drive onto the highway in a frenzy of dust and raced away. She had seen that he was fairly tall and under the typical cowboy hat was a very straight roman nose and a nice mustache. She could tell little else.

J.D., clad in her usual western shirt, levis, and boots joined the boys in their baseball game without a backward glance. Why, Alecia wondered, was J.D. the only student at Charlesy School who didn't ride the bus?

The boys seemed content to have her in their midst and Mr. Jenkins instructed her in methods to improve her pitch. From her window vantage point, Alecia could see J.D.'s brown eyes growing wide with appreciation at the instructions.

Alecia glanced at the white-face pendulum clock above the chalkboard. Flossie Cramer, the teacher of the first and second grades, would soon be ringing the bell. Alecia drew herself away from the window and returned to her desk to review the day's lesson plans.

Charlesy School, the last of its kind in the area, couldn't be considered a full elementary school, for it accommodated first through sixth grades only. Two classes were housed in each classroom. The huge stone edifice, which overlooked the pasturelands, also held a small library, a school office, a spacious lunchroom, and a gymnasium with a stage at one end.

Flossie, the paradox of a teacher dressed in a slogan tee shirt and levis, and no more than two years out of college, stuck her head in Alecia's classroom doorway. "Brace yourself, Babe. It's time." The brass bell was cupped over her hand as she held the clapper in silence.

"I'm ready." Alecia's response was cool. Her years of

training in the Minneapolis school system made her recoil at Flossie's unprofessional approach to teaching.

With great clompings, clatterings, and chatterings, the third- and fourth-graders converged on Alecia's classroom. During her years in and out of classroom situations, she had never taught two grade levels simultaneously. It was proving to be a greater challenge than she had ever imagined.

In the midst of the noise, she looked up to see J.D. standing before her desk holding out a fistful of wildflowers. The girl's brown eyes were wide and expectant.

"Why, thank you, J.D. These are lovely." Alecia motioned for her to come nearer and gave her a brief hug.

"I knew you'd like them," the girl announced. "Miss Cramer would have called them old weeds."

Yes, that sounded like Flossie, Alecia thought as she instructed J.D. to fetch a vase of water for the blossoms. During the course of the day, Alecia found herself, as usual, involuntarily observing J.D. at her work. The girl's careful habits belied the tomboy exterior. Generally, girls with tomboy tendencies were prone to be lax in neatness, but such wasn't the case with J.D. All her lessons were completed with precision.

Mrs. Dominique, the Charlesy School cook of twenty years, teased students and staff alike during the morning hours with fragrant aromas of baking lasagna. At noon, Alecia remained in her room for a few moments of work after dismissing her students for their lunch hour. By the time she entered the lunch room, Flossie and Mrs. Turner, the school secretary, were leaving. Alecia filled her tray and seated herself beside Lyle Jenkins, thankful to find him alone.

"Hello, Miss Winland," he greeted her, assisting with

her full tray. "I must say, you're looking very nice today." With an unconcealed chuckle, he added, "A refreshing respite from Flossie's faded blue jeans."

Alecia smiled her thanks, remembering what her sister, Nancy, had said to her that morning about being "over-dressed" for Charlesy School. Actually, the tailored suit was on a par with everything else in her closet. She hadn't much choice.

She let a few meaningless generalities sift back and forth before asking the question foremost on her mind—that of J.D. and her background.

"I don't know all that much about the Lassiters," Lyle admitted. "Rayne, J.D.'s father, is a successful rancher. . .a widower I believe. As you have no doubt surmised, there's not much feminine influence for J.D."

"That's what concerns me."

"Isn't she doing well in class?"

"Academically, I see no problems," Alecia explained. "But socially I can detect problems. She's developing very few relationships with the girls her age."

Lyle smiled. "J.D.'s just her daddy's little ranch hand."

Alecia bristled at his nonchalance. "How unfair. It may interest you to know that a few days ago, I found J.D. sketching pictures during free time. Pictures of elegant ladies in long flowing dresses. Is she being a little ranch hand against her will?"

Lyle cleared his throat. "Now Miss Winland, these people out here are very set in their ways. I'm sure J.D.'s as happy as she can be. If she were disturbed about something, it would show up in her school work."

"Not necessarily," Alecia countered.

"Excuse me. I keep forgetting your background in child psychology and counseling."

Alecia detected his condescending tone was to humor her, but she let it pass. "I think she's unhappy inside, and I'd go so far as to say she's under duress at having to conform to a mold that someone else is forming for her." Someone such as a stern rancher-father who drives a blue pickup, she silently surmised, who won't allow his daughter to ride the bus. Although the lasagna was delicious, Alecia found she couldn't finish eating.

Lyle thoughtfully rolled his water glass between his palms. "I admire your sensitivity and your concern," he said slowly, "but you'll learn these ranchers are different from people you and I have known."

This was the first hint she had received that someone here was as urban as she was. He continued, "There's an element of underlying pride and individuality that is an unwritten law. It's the code by which Rayne Lassiter and his daughter live. We can be appreciative and sympathetic, but I've found there's nothing you or I can do to change their ways."

Alecia didn't answer, but she had witnessed that individuality he referred to in Nancy. Almost twenty years Alecia's senior, Nancy, during her widowhood, and now during her recovery from major surgery, was indomitable in her determination to hold on to her small ranch.

The sisters had not been reared with such fortitude and love of land. Their lives had been very urban, even though it was small town urban. They were more familiar with sidewalks, storefronts, and shade trees than with open spaces and cattle branding. Alecia could only surmise that Nancy had acquired her stamina and persistence during her years of marriage to rancher, Ted Whitlow.

But Alecia didn't voice these thoughts. People aren't that different, really, no matter where they live, she told herself. And it still remained that a little girl like J.D. needed a helping hand.

When she looked up to speak again, Lyle was standing to leave. "I'll have to ask you to confine your interests to the classroom, Miss Winland," he told her. This was her superior speaking now. "I appreciate your expertise in other areas of education, but it won't pay for you to use those talents here."

Thoroughly miffed, Alecia dumped her remaining lunch in the garbage can. Too late, she saw Mrs. Dominique peering over her glasses at her with a disgusted gaze that should have been reserved for the students.

That afternoon, J.D.'s usual animation became subdued, and her face was pale. Her brown eyes beneath closely cropped curls appeared larger and wider than ever. Presently, she approached Alecia's desk. Clutching her stomach, she said, "Take me home, Miss Winland. I don't feel so good."

"I'm sorry you don't feel well, J.D. Is you father home? We can call him."

"He might be home, but he's never at the house," she answered, wincing.

"But J.D., I can't leave the classroom."

She brightened. "Mrs. Turner can substitute. She's used to it."

"Very well. Return to your desk. I'll talk to Mr. Jenkins about it. Are you sure you can't make it till school is out?"

Clutching at her stomach again, J.D. shook her head.

A few minutes later, Alecia was standing at the door of Lyle's classroom, feeling a bit foolish for asking for permission to take J.D. home.

"The school policy," Lyle explained, not unkindly, "is for Mrs. Turner to take students home when necessary."

"I know the policy," she replied. She could scarcely believe her own words. She was never one to break policies of any kind. "But J.D. seems to have attached herself to me and has asked me to take her." Blindly, she let emotions plunge on, ignoring the bite of conscience. "Surely it couldn't hurt anything. I believe the child needs an ally."

"Obviously your mind is set, thinking you can do something positive in J.D.'s life. I don't fault you for that, Miss Winland. I just don't want to see you get hurt."

"Are you letting me go?"

Lyle nodded. "Against my better judgement."

"Thank you," she answered, then left before he could change his mind.

Although J.D. was cheered to know her teacher would be driving her home, it was clear the girl was genuinely sick. Mrs. Turner came in to take Alecia's place, as the two of them left before the afternoon recess. J.D. climbed into Alecia's car, running her small hands over the creamy upholstery and admiring the dashboard. Alecia smiled. What a captivating little personality she was.

Nothing could have prepared Alecia for the El Crosse Ranch. For several miles along the narrow road, J. D. was pointing to the rolling hills dotted with passive grazing cattle saying, "That's our land there." Finally, there was an open gate of sturdy white wood with a massive sign above announcing: EL CROSSE RANCH, with the running L brand burned into each corner. A meandering drive flanked by trim white rail fences and gracefully arched mimosa trees beckoned to them. The mimosas sported fresh pink feather blossoms that waved softly in the breeze.

"Go on, Miss Winland," J.D. urged, bouncing in the

seat. "Go on in. This is where I live."

The drive took them up a long steady incline. At the break of the hill, Alecia was stunned to survey the scene below. Spread out across a broad, shallow valley were more than a half-dozen outbuildings, barns, stables, and tall silos crowned with silver domes reflecting the azure sky. The area was cross-fenced with the same neat white fences as those that lined the drive.

The sprawling, white Spanish-styled home lay at the forefront of the panoramic view. The lawn was graced by large, shady oaks, and rainbow flower beds.

From J.D.'s few comments about having to help her daddy on the ranch, Alecia had assumed it was the two of them struggling alone. However, there were several men working down by the corral as she pulled to a stop in front of the house.

A measure of J.D.'s animation was coming back to life. "There he is, Miss Winland. There's my daddy. Down by the corral, working the cattle."

"Shall I drive down?"

"No, ma'am," she said, jumping out. "I'll call him."

When she gave her whoop, all the men looked in their direction but only one, taller than the rest, climbed down from the white fence and moved toward them with purposeful strides. Alecia lifted her sunglasses from her eyes and perched them atop her windblown hair as she stood beside the car. Suddenly, she felt very ill at ease.

It was with great delight that J.D. introduced her teacher to her father. Alecia found herself looking up into a handsome bronzed face set with J.D.'s expressive, brown eyes. There was the straight nose and trim mustache she had observed from the school window. He took off his hat and reached for her hand. "Rayne Lassiter, ma'am. Pleased to meet you. You're Nancy Whitlow's sister. How's she doing?"

"Nancy's doing better now, thank you." Alecia's hand, strengthened by numerous racquetball and tennis games, felt a strength in his grasp far surpassing hers. "J.D. wasn't feeling well. She, uh, she said you couldn't be reached by phone."

Rayne gave his daughter a stern look as he released Alecia's hand. "I can see you're feeling bad, J.D.," he said softly, "but is that an excuse to story?"

"No, sir."

"You knew Josie would be in the house, didn't you?"

"Yes, sir," came the meek reply.

"And that she could have reached me on the barn phone or the two-way units?"

"Yes." J.D. hung her head, but Alecia could see a slight smile at the corners of her mouth.

Barn phones? Two-way units? Was someone pulling her leg? And who was Josie? Suddenly, Alecia found herself wishing Mrs. Turner had brought J.D. home.

At that moment the front door of the house opened and a gray-haired woman clad in blue jeans, stepped briskly toward them. "My lands, little gal. What're you doing home?"

"Sick, Josie," J.D. replied—the validity of which Alecia now began to doubt. "Meet my teacher, Miss Winland."

Josie's manner was a good deal softer than her leathery old face indicated. Following the introductions, she whisked J.D. into the house.

Rayne, meanwhile, was apologetic. Unhooking a thumb from his belt loop, he jabbed it toward the corral. "Excuse me, Miss Winland, but I've got to get back to work. Sorry J.D. told you that fib about phoning. Guess she was impressed by your pretty little sports car there. Just wanted a ride."

The grandeur of the ranch had almost rendered Alecia speechless, but now she was regaining her professional composure. She had come all this way and didn't intend to be dismissed so quickly. J.D. was more important than cows.

"Rayne, you have a lovely daughter," she said with more boldness than she was feeling under the gaze of the intense brown eyes. "I've been watching her, and though it's none of my business, I thought you should know some of the kids tease her because of the way she dresses."

The tall cowboy straightened himself and said nothing. Alecia swallowed and continued. "When I stopped in Kalado the other day, I saw a dress in Archer's window I'm sure J.D. would adore. With your permission, I'd like to get it for her as a gift. Even if she only wore a dress once in a while."

All the words she had prepared suddenly sounded empty in view of the Lassiters' lifestyle. Her eyes strayed to several large horse trailers in front of the stables with the running L brand, and the words EL CROSSE RANCH in elegant white swirls against the deep blue.

When she glanced back, Rayne's face had gone cold and distant. "If you'd been observing more closely," he remarked, "you'd see that J.D. is the happiest girl in Denlin County. Standing up for what she believes will make her stronger. Now, if you'll excuse me."

Alecia never intended to press him, but why couldn't he see what he was doing to this sensitive child? Short hair, no name, boys' clothes. Ridiculous! "I've seen her sketching pictures of ladies in dresses, Mr. Lassiter," she said, "so they are on her mind. Feminine things are a valid necessity in her life."

Rayne replaced his Stetson, casting a shadow across his somber face. "Miss Teacher Lady, how about if you quietly finish out the school year, then go back and use your high class psychology on those poor city folk who live so close together their brains are tied in knots. We manage to do fine without it, thank you."

She was surprised he knew her background, and yet she shouldn't have been. News spread like a pasture fire in Denlin County. "It's not psychology," she retorted, barely able to cap her indignation. "I'm talking about plain old common sense. Surely you can see that."

But the resistance she had encountered was hard as an Oklahoma dirt clod in August. Mr. Rayne Lassiter tipped his hat and slowly walked away with an easy loose-jointed gait, leaving her fuming.

She slipped behind the wheel and slammed the door of her car with more force than intended. In all her years in the field of education—teaching, administrating, counseling, working with gifted students—never had she made a scene with the parent of a student. What had gotten into her?

She turned the key in the ignition. There was a whining noise, a groan, then nothing. She tried again. Nothing. She was desperate for a quick exit. She felt the heat of her flushed cheeks. How could she let him unnerve her so? Rayne was nearly down to the corral. Surely he could hear the car failing to start, but he kept walking.

She would have to phone Lyle at the school. How humiliating, after she had gone against school policy to come here. "This is what I get, isn't it, Lord?" she muttered, "for asserting myself with this father with no preliminary planning." One last time, she turned the key and accelerated ruthlessly. The engine repeated its pathetic groan.

Down at the white-fenced corral, Alecia watched as Rayne motioned to one of his men to follow him. As he neared her car again, she could see his half-smile that irritated her.

"Pull the hood latch," Rayne instructed her.

Alecia reached down and jerked at a handle, then paused to listen for the click of the hood latch. Looking down, she realized she had pulled the emergency brake handle that wasn't even engaged. She glanced up. Rayne stood there waiting. The other cowboy, who was thinner and more grizzled, grinned at her as he chewed on a match stick. His greasy cowboy hat was curled up on the edges like a dried leaf in autumn.

"The hood?" Rayne repeated.

"Just a minute. I'm getting it." She grabbed the correct handle and the hood gave its releasing pop. She replaced her sunglasses on her nose to hide her embarrassment.

"Sammy," Rayne instructed his worker, "get in and give it a turn."

Doesn't even trust me to start my own car, she thought with disgust, as she slipped over to the rider's side. He must think her a total dunce. She should have protested, but she didn't have the strength. All she wanted now was to get the car started and leave.

Sammy grinned again as he folded his rangy legs into her small car. Alecia cringed as the muddy boots touched the eggshell carpeting.

"Hey, boss," Sammy said, "if this is the new shape of Charlesy's faculty, we'd better get up to some of them PTA meetings."

Ignoring his obvious flirt, Alecia managed to retort

calmly, "We'd be pleased to have you at the PTA meetings, Sammy. The school certainly needs more community involvement."

"It's the choke, Sammy," Rayne called from beneath the hood. "Didn't kick in. Try it now."

Deftly, Sammy turned the key and effortlessly the engine sprang to life and purred like one of Nancy's barn cats.

"Traitor," Alecia accused it under her breath.

Sammy crawled back out, leaving the remains of various-sized dirt clods around the gas pedal. At least she hoped it was dirt. Now that she had spent time in the feed lots and corrals, she knew what boots could carry.

Disguising her exasperation beneath a thin veil of calm, she scooted behind the wheel and declared a partially sane "Thank you" to the two men.

She expected a cynical accusation to be flung back at her, and was relieved when Rayne simply touched his hat and nodded. "Think nothing of it," he said.

Beside him, Sammy grinned silly and spat out match stick splinters. Rayne turned to his ranch hand and shook his head before the two of them ambled back down toward the corral.

Gone was Alecia's heated desire to spin tires and spit fine white gravel into the air. Cautiously, she guided her car down the long drive and waited until she had passed the white gate of the El Crosse entrance before pouring it on. She put quick miles between her and that humiliating experience.

Even though she knew it was her own disobedience that put her there, Alecia hoped she would never have occasion to visit El Crosse again. Why was it that anytime she became uncomfortable here, it caused her to miss Minneapolis more than ever?

"For I have learned, in whatsoever state I am, therewith to be content," she repeated to the wind whipping in the window. "I have learned. I have learned." She shook her head and moaned. "No, I haven't, Lord. I haven't learned at all. And I want to go home in the worst way."

two

Thankfully, the bus was gone when Alecia returned to the school to pick up a stack of papers to grade that evening. Tomorrow would be soon enough to answer Lyle's inevitable question of, "How did it go?"

Surely by morning she would think up a sensible answer to give him. Sensible. That was a word she often chose when describing her own personality traits. And never before had she acted more irrationally. As she headed out the door with a stuffed folder, she was startled to hear sounds in the next room. Peeking around the door frame, she was surprised to see Flossie still in her classroom. Usually, the childlike woman was the first to vacate the premises.

"Hello, Flossie," she said, wishing she had kept walking right out the front door. "Working on lesson plans?"

"Gosh no! I'm waiting for Lonnie Wayne to come and get me." She nibbled at the edge of a candy bar. "We're driving into Kalado for something to eat, then to a movie. He said he might even take me dancing at Tiggles afterwards. Lonnie Wayne's quite a spender." Flossie gave a vague smile and hooked her straight hair over an ear. "How'd you make out at the Lassiters'? That Rayne's a real hunk, isn't he?"

The question caught Alecia off guard. "Hunk?"

"He's a lot of man, honey. Three-fourths of Denlin County's female population would give a right arm to talk to him, but Rayne keeps mostly to himself. Smart move

20

for you to get Lyle to let you take the kid home so you could meet him. Wish I'd thought of it."

"Flossie, really. Keep your imagination under control." Alecia couldn't deny her curiosity that morning as Rayne drove up to let J.D. out at school, but it was by no means a romantic curiosity. She wanted to see the kind of man who would dress such a precious little girl in boys' clothes and call her by ambiguous initials.

"I underestimated you," Flossie went on. "Beneath that high-sheen surface beats the heart of your everyday man-chaser. Welcome to the club."

"I'm late," Alecia said, not wanting to be put on the defensive any further. "Nancy will be wondering where I am. See you in the morning."

"Sure thing, Alecia." Flossie took another bite of the candy bar, letting bits of chocolate and peanuts fall to the cluttered desk. "Don't work too hard." Her wave indicated the folder. "Nobody here will be impressed if you do."

Alecia left in silence. No reply was needed. Why, she wondered as she turned the car out of the school parking lot, was that girl even allowed to teach? Flossie's lacka-daisical attitude toward her work grated on Alecia's nerves. Apparently, there were no constructive solutions she could propose to Lyle or the school board in the few remaining weeks of the school term. But she was concerned for the first- and second-graders who daily sat under Flossie's teaching.

The tension in Alecia's neck and shoulders did not begin to ebb until she turned off the highway onto the section line road leading to Nancy's ranch. The hay meadows were greening and the cottonwoods decked out in delicate fringes and miniature leaves. The willows, draping over their farm pond reflections, had been the very first to leaf out and were in full dress. For all the blessings of an early spring, Alecia still longed for the familiar surroundings of downtown Minneapolis.

Delia, her roommate back home, had laughed out loud over the phone when Alecia told her about hiring on at Charlesy School a week ago.

"A country school? Wait'll Superintendent Harwood hears about this," she said. Delia, a marketing analyst, was such a realist. "I didn't know such things still existed."

"There're a few around still gasping for breath. The job was all Nancy's idea," she defended herself. "She was afraid I might pace a hole in the living room carpet. When the opening became available, she practically threw me into it. She called the school and told the principal I could fill in till the end of the term."

Delia laughed again in her deep throaty laugh. "What happened to the other teacher? Catch her hair in the threshing machine?"

"Delia, be nice! Actually, she eloped and ran off to Louisiana." But Alecia could hardly find fault with Delia's "country" jokes when she stood guilty of making a few private ones herself.

Before reaching the Whitlow Ranch, the country road dipped down around a series of curves, where a small mobile home was situated in a shaded glen. Alecia could see Jake Shanks sitting outside, with his straight-back chair tilted back against the side of the trailer. She slowed her car to a stop at the side of the road. The old man's felt hat, more battered even than Sammy's, was slouched down over his face.

"Jake!" she called out, rousing him from his nap. The chair dropped to the ground with a thud, and he pushed his hat to the back of his head.

"Hey there, Miss Winland." He waved a half-full whiskey bottle in the air at her. He seemed to keep a solid grip on it even while napping. His wrinkled face spread into a wide smile.

"Nancy asked me to stop and ask if you can come by and fix the south fence sometime soon. She says it's too weak to hold back Roscoe if he starts eyeing the Domiers' heifers."

"Be pleased to assist two such lovely ladies, Miss Winland." Jake rose on unsteady, bowed legs. "Tell her I'll be by soon. We'll keep that old bull where he belongs. Say, how're you doing with the feeding now?"

"Better. Thanks to your effective teaching." Alecia smiled as she remembered how Jake patiently took her through each step of feeding Nancy's livestock at the various feeding stations when she arrived in mid-February. Nancy was still in the hospital then.

"For a city gal, you're turning out to be a good hand. As soon as you get the hang of it, you'll go and leave us." Jake pulled off the companionable hat and smoothed down his scraggly gray hair.

Alecia stepped from her car and crossed the road to where Jake was standing. She caught the sweet fragrance of the black locust trees in bloom. "Looks that way," she said. "Nancy's stronger each day. I'm sure she won't need me much longer. But I'll stay till the end of the school term."

Suddenly, the blast of a horn caught Alecia off balance. A beige double-cab pickup with bright red pinstriping and matching horse trailer in tow came barreling through the curves. She immediately recognized Corrine Domier, Nancy's neighbor to the south. The blast sounded again and instinctively, Alecia stepped toward the ditch and felt her good suede pumps sink into the soft spring mud.

Corrine sped by with not so much as a nod in their direction. Her brilliant red hair was fastened at the nape of her neck beneath a pale blue western hat.

As the pickup whizzed past, Jake loped over to give her a hand. "You all right, Miss Winland?" he asked as he grabbed for her arm. "No need to dive for the ditch. Them trees woulda protected you." Shaking his head, he muttered, "Them two Lamison sisters used to be the sweetest girls in the county."

Gratefully, Alecia let Jake assist her back to her car. "Thanks, Jake. Has that woman got a problem?"

"Not that I know of. Plenty of money and plenty of good looks. She's just one of them determined women."

Of all the friendly ranchers Alecia had met in the area, the Domiers alone had chosen to remain aloof. Alecia was introduced to the couple once, and once was enough. The beautiful Corrine was cool and distant. Her husband, Lavren, had seemed almost frightening to Alecia as he looked at her with steel gray eyes that seemed to want to possess all they surveyed.

Gingerly, she removed her muddy shoes and placed them bottom-side-up on the floor before getting in her car. "Thanks again," she told him, "for everything."

"T'weren't nothing." He closed the door after she was settled. "Give Mrs. Whitlow my respects."

How gentle he was. How sad that he should waste his life away, living alone and nursing bottle after bottle of booze.

Arriving at Nancy's house, Alecia was struck at how differently the Whitlow Ranch appeared after seeing the immensity of El Crosse. Nancy's spacious brick, ranch-styled home, edged with trim shrubs, seemed miniature in comparison to the rambling stucco home of Rayne Lassiter. And she was certain she had seen only a portion of El Crosse.

The early spring air was cooling as she turned into the drive and that convinced her to roll up the car windows before going in. From one day to the next, one could never predict the Oklahoma weather.

Aromas that greeted her in the front hall told her Nancy had chicken cooking. No yogurt and salad suppers here.

"You're late," Nancy called to her from the den at the back of the house.

"Had errands to run." She slipped out of her muddy shoes at the door and strode stocking-footed out to the den.

Nancy had a small fire going in the glass-fronted woodburning stove. She was settled in the wing-backed chair with a book and a cup of coffee. "Come on in," she said cheerily, "get comfy and tell me about your day. Cup of coffee?"

"Thanks, Sis, but I'd better change and get the chores done first." Alecia stopped a moment and studied her sister's tired face. "Nancy, you look beat. What's the matter?"

Nancy failed to mask her sheepish smile.

"Okay. Out with it. What major task did our recuperating patient undertake today?" It had been close to impossible to keep Nancy down and resting according to doctor's orders. Her determination to keep the ranch in tiptop condition was a driving force.

"It was such a lovely day, and I can't be expected to just sit around."

"Come on. Quit stalling."

"The tomato plants. I set them out."

"All fifteen of them?"

Nancy's smile broadened with satisfaction. "All fifteen!" Though her usually ruddy cheeks were lacking their normal color, the sense of accomplishment gave her an inner glow.

"I could have helped you on Saturday," Alecia chided. She lay the folder down on the card table they had set up as her work area. "You should have waited."

"You've done so much already. You dropped everything to come and be with me. I suppose I'll never fully appreciate the magnitude of the project you were working on with Galen. It overwhelms me to think you released it all to come and be an underpaid ranch hand." Her eyes twinkled. "The least I can do is care for a small garden."

Alecia chafed at Nancy's words, for not a day passed that she didn't struggle with those very thoughts. It had been a sacrifice to leave it all—her cozy apartment, the project with gifted students, the city she knew and loved, Delia, Galen. . . . And yet she loved her older sister with an unspeakable love.

Nancy's mention of the gifted children's program stirred her ever present heart's cry to get on with that vital work rather than sitting here in rural America growing stagnant. Stagnant! That was it! She felt stifled and useless here. She longed to be back where she was needed the most. Alecia knelt down and opened the doors of the stove and shook down the charring logs with a poker. She hoped her sister couldn't read her thoughts by her expression.

"And by the way," Nancy said, seemingly oblivious, "don't forget, on Saturday we're attending the Field Day at the Research Station."

"Wow! A step up the social ladder in Denlin County. Gracious, is my feathered Stetson back from the cleaners?" She rose and swung the poker around. "Let me see, do I carry my branding iron in the left or right hand?" She pranced across the den as Nancy chuckled at her antics.

"Joke if you will, but there's an element of social life in this county that would surprise you. Anyway, this is just a Field Day that will end up with a barbecue at one of the area's ranches. The agents will be showing several pasture grasses under experimentation. I'm anxious to learn how to get my northeast pasture in full production next summer. It was nowhere near as lush as it could have been last year."

"By all means then, to the Field Day it is. And now I've got to get out here and take care of all those things that feed on that lush pasture."

Nancy stood up. "I'll get the pickup around."

Alecia stepped quickly and put a firm hand on her sister's shoulder. "You'll do no such thing. Digging in the garden was enough for you today. We'll never get you well if you don't slow down."

Nancy's clear laugh rang out as she sank back down. "Okay, okay. I declare, if you keep worrying about me, you'll have an ulcer. Get on out there, and I'll get supper on."

In her room, Alecia quickly changed into blue jeans, a shirt, and boots. Wouldn't Delia have a convulsion if she ever saw this outfit. But Alecia learned quickly that close-fitting western shirts were less binding beneath a jacket while riding. And to round up calves in anything but boots was ludicrous. Especially after Jake told her that rattlers go for the ankle!

Sparkie, Nancy's sheltie collie, met Alecia at the back door, ready and anxious for work. Alecia rubbed the ruff of copper-colored fur around the dog's neck. "Good girl.

Let's get these chores done." Sparkie happily trotted ahead of her toward the barns.

New tomato plants peeked bright green fingers through the dark soil of the garden. Alecia remember Nancy's sadness as she lay in the hospital, being unable to get her seed potatoes planted. Alecia shook her head in bewilderment at her sister's motivation in the mundane.

She checked the automatic feeders and waterers, then tended to three orphaned calves who had to be fed from the buckets with nipples fastened to the bottom. She hurried through the series of chores to get to her favorite—caring for the horses.

Before Ted Whitlow died, the stables were stocked with several high quality quarter horses. Nancy was forced to sell most of them, but had kept the exquisite stallion, Raisin Kane, and the mare, Kane Brake. Then there was old Peppy, the solid cow pony who was a worker deluxe. Peppy had been a godsend when Alecia first helped Jake bring up steers for sale.

There was a sense of peace and order in the stable. The fragrances of hay, leather, and horses were strangely comforting. Over the stalls, Alecia spoke to each horse and stroked velvety muzzles. Kane Brake was a brilliant mare, and already Alecia adored her. Peppy was accommodating, but Kane Brake was regal.

"Good girl," Alecia cooed to her. "Back up there a minute. Let me get this feed in here. What you need is a good workout, don't you? You and I'll have to start taking long evening rides."

Kane Brake pushed against her shoulder as she worked. For a moment, Alecia stopped and lay her head against the long gentle face as though to soak up the peace and patience dwelling there.

How much longer? she wondered. So much work to be done back home. Galen needed her. Why all the stopping and waiting? "Sure, Lord," she whispered, "if I had nothing else in the world to do, I couldn't think of a place I'd rather be, but—"

Abruptly, Kane Brake pulled back from her grasp and shook her head, nickering a scolding for the pity party Alecia was having. She laughed. "Okay, okay, I know. Be thankful for everything. Right? Funny, but I'm usually the one telling that to other people." Stepping out of the stall, she gave the gracious mare one more pat. "Thanks for the consultation, Kane Brake. Have the bill sent to my address. Come on, Sparkie," she called. "We'd better take a look at the south fence for Nancy."

The sheltie raced her to the pickup. As they bounced along across the pasture, she wondered if she would recognize a fence in need of repair when she saw it. Actually, she wasn't sure what she was looking for. Later, she realized she needn't have worried. The fence along the gully was loose and drooping. And this was the pasture where Roscoe, the bull, was spending his time. Either the fence would have to be repaired soon or all the cows and heifers would have to be moved to another pasture.

Jake had explained to Alecia that the Domiers raised brangus cattle, a cross breed of angus and Brahmas. Should Roscoe, a polled Hereford, break through that fence, it would spell big trouble for the Domier herd.

She brought the pickup to a halt and stepped out to gaze across the vast expanse of land before her. The stout prairie wind whipped around her. Scissor-tailed flycatchers played tag in the air and the killdeer gave their little screeches as they scurried through the grass near their ill-concealed nests.

The grass was a dull gray-brown when Alecia first arrived in Oklahoma. Now, a new birth of green life was coming forth. The land was so different from the Minnesota countryside. What was it that had compelled early day settlers to remain here? They must have had eyes of faith to envision putting roots down in the sunbaked, wind-swept prairie.

The sound of horse's hooves behind her startled her. She turned to see a rider approaching from the Domier Ranch. Presently, she recognized Lavren himself astride his silver gelding. Alecia had often seen the rancher from a distance working with his men. Premature graying hair gave him a distinguished look, but his gray eyes were ice cold.

A soft growl came from where Sparkie lay beneath the truck. "Quiet, girl," Alecia ordered.

Lavren's gelding was reined to a halt at the fence. He surprised her by moving the mount close to the fence and dismounting on the Whitlow side. "Fence inspecting, Miss Winland?" He stepped purposefully toward her. As before, the harsh gray eyes looked her over.

A shiver ran from Alecia's arm to her neck. Sparkie growled again. "Nancy mentioned it might be weak here. She's having it fixed in a few days."

"In a few days? That might be too late." The voice was as cold as the eyes. "Better advise your sister of that fact. She seems to be growing forgetful of late. She knows this stretch of fence is Whitlow responsibility and I expect it to be fixed before that renegade bull of hers gets over into my brangus heifers." Intermittently, he flicked the riding quirt in his hand against his leg.

Alecia knew for a fact that since Ted died, the Atwoods, whose land butted the Whitlow Ranch to the east and north, willingly helped Nancy keep fences in repair. But

Lavren Domier obviously never considered extending such favors.

"My sister, Mr. Domier, is recuperating from major surgery. She's regaining her strength and is attempting to keep everything under control. She's aware of the fence and is seeing to its repair." Alecia felt the strain to keep the tremor from her voice. "That should be sufficient."

"Mrs. Whitlow's physical condition is none of my concern. My cattle are. If I find that bull in my pasture, your sister could own a dead bull."

A swell of anger rose in Alecia's midsection. "I hardly call that fair," she snapped. "The fence will be fixed. What more do you want?"

"Assurance." He moved nearer. "That my herd won't be ruined by an infirmed widow running a ranch from her sickbed. And if she's hired that soakhead Shanks to do it, I have no assurance."

Alecia could never remember feeling rage like that which was now rising to a frenzied peak. She wanted to grab his quirt and slap him across his proud face. Nancy was anything but an infirmed widow. This man had to be demented. "Mr. Domier, you happen to be on Whitlow land at this moment. I'll thank you to take your crude expressions and degrading remarks and get out of here!"

The rancher's face relaxed into a sardonic smile. "You're very attractive, Miss Winland. This ranch life is certainly no place for someone like you." He reached out and placed one lone finger on her cheek and let it trail slowly under her chin to lift it slightly.

Disgusted, Alecia raised her hand to land one solid slap, but Lavren was quicker and caught her wrist, squeezing it hard. At the sound of her sharp cry, Sparkie sprang from beneath the pickup and sank bared teeth into Lavren's soft

leg, just above the boot top. The expensive pants gave way
with a rip as Lavren jumped back while trying to strike at
Sparkie with the quirt. "Get away from me, you mutt. Call
off this dog! Call him off!" Struggling, he tried to get to
the fence, dragging the tenacious animal with him.

"Sparkie!" Alecia commanded. "Stay, Sparkie."

The cool Mr. Domier was now extremely heated up.
Alecia could see the jaws set in anger. Free from the dog,
he jumped the drooping fence and mounted the waiting
gelding. Momentarily, he glanced back. "Tell you sister
what I said. And I'll send a bill for the pants."

When he was gone, Alecia knelt down and hugged
Sparkie in sheer relief. "Really sent him sailing, didn't
you, girl? Thanks."

Suddenly, Alecia felt a gnawing concern for Nancy's
safety. Her sister who had practically reared her—the one
so solid in faith and strong in all circumstances—now
seemed pitifully vulnerable.

Later that evening when she related the incident to
Nancy, her sister was quite cool about it.

"That Lavren," she scoffed. "He's more bark than bite.
Don't give it another thought, Alecia. I'm sorry if he
disturbed you."

Alecia didn't argue, nor did she explain that he had
touched her. Nancy had lived here for many years. She
ought to know if the man was harmless or not. But inwardly,
Alecia still maintained that those steel gray eyes indicated
more than a biteless bark.

Another one of Nancy's marvelous suppers nearly erased
from Alecia's mind the encounters with the two very
different men that day. After the dishwasher was loaded,
she took her papers into the den in front of the crackling fire
where Nancy was fussing over financial records.

The fire whispered as they worked, wrapped in their individual blankets of thought. Alecia knew she would miss the fire when the days grew warmer. It had, at first, been such a bother to carry in wood and tote out ashes that flew everywhere before she could get the ash pan out the door. But when Nancy was still in the hospital, Alecia chose to sleep on the den sofa because of the warmth and company of the fire.

On top of the stack of school papers on the table was J.D.'s math assignment. Alecia smiled. Each problem was evenly spaced and neatly written. It struck her afresh that this was not the work of a carefree tomboytype. She had done enough counseling to recognize that.

"Alecia." Nancy's voice cut into the quiet. "You never told me why you were late this afternoon. Some errand you said."

Alecia looked up from J.D.'s paper feeling as though Nancy were reading her thoughts. "One of my students became ill and I took her home."

"Anyone I know?"

"I thought you knew everyone," Alecia joked. "It was the Lassiters at the El Crosse Ranch. They call the little girl J.D."

"J.D.? She's in third grade already?" Nancy took a sip from her coffee mug. "I can hardly believe it. Seems like she was a toddler just yesterday. What did you think of their ranch? Something isn't it? Second biggest in the county."

"Unbelievable." Cautiously, she asked, "Are you very well acquainted with the family?"

"As well as anyone in a small community. You know about people, but do any of us really know one another? What did you want to know?"

Alecia paused. She wanted to know so much. Everything. "How did J.D.'s mother die?" That would do for starters.

"It was a fire. Five years ago."

"Burned to death? How awful. Where? How?"

"I don't know all the details." Nancy returned her attention to the calculator in her hand. "It's one of those things people want to forget."

It sounded to Alecia like one of those things people would always remember. "Mr. Lassiter asked about you. Do you know him well?"

"Rayne? Through business is all." She poked figures into the calculator. "He taught me a few things about breeding the heifers after Ted died. Ted knew him better than I did." She looked up. "The El Crosse belonged to Rayne's father, Roland, and I imagine it belonged to his father before him. When Rayne married, his father gave him the ranch house, and he moved into a smaller one there on the ranch."

"The name El Crosse, does that mean. . . ."

"That they're Christians? No, Honey, I don't think so. Seems to me the story goes that the ranch was situated at the crossroads of two cattle drive trails, so they simply put the cross in the loop of the L and made the name, El Crosse."

Alecia felt a twinge of disappointment. Had Rayne Lassiter been a Christian, perhaps there would be an avenue of communication there. Oh well. "I'm a little concerned about J.D.," she said aloud after a moment.

"In what way?"

"Her father seems to be rearing her like one of the ranch hands. Short hair, work clothes. He doesn't let her ride the bus. He doesn't even use her name. It disturbs me."

Nancy continued entering figures into the calculator. "She's in good hands. Her daddy's crazy about her."

"Let's not be naive. Surely you're aware of what overprotection can do to the normal development of a child."

"Ranchers are different from people you're accustomed to, Alecia. There's an intrinsic pride—a vein of survival instinct—that has been ingrained through the years," Nancy pointed out. "I'm sure Rayne feels he's doing every possible good thing for his daughter."

There it was again. The excuse that ranchers are somehow different from the rest of society. Alecia shuffled papers and made a few red pencil jots. "Pride can easily disguise selfishness," she intoned flatly.

Nancy smiled her heartwarming smile. "But we can't really be the judge, now can we?"

Alecia knew from experience that the case was closed as far as Nancy was concerned. As usual, her sister's sweet disposition put her to shame.

Later in the evening, they brought out their Bibles and shared their usual devotion and prayer time together. The logs made a soft shuffling sound as they settled down in the ashes, as Nancy read the Scriptures. Though cultures and miles had separated the two sisters for years, their corporate love of God drew them together in an inseparable bond.

Later, alone in her room, Alecia once again thought about her confrontation with Rayne that afternoon. If only she had used wisdom and patience. Why was she so overly concerned about a child she might never see again after two months? Perhaps it was an outgrowth of the restlessness she was experiencing at having to stay here.

Thoughtfully, she sat on the edge of the bed brushing her hair. She wanted to have a peaceable spirit. She wanted to be able to look at people and circumstances through eyes of patient love. And yet she had been guilty of letting her emotions rule. She wanted to apologize to Rayne and begin again. But how? She was sure he had given her no more thought than to a pesky horsefly.

"Give it up," she scolded herself as she changed into her gown and slipped between the cool sheets. "Teach the children at Charlesy School, finish the term quietly, and get back to Minneapolis where you belong."

She fell asleep by turning her thoughts to Galen Rustin, their work together, and his dependable tenderness toward her.

three

The next morning, when Alecia arrived at Charlesy, Flossie was seated on the broad concrete ledge beside the school steps, swinging her legs and chewing gum. Alecia made a determined effort to be friendly, smiling as she approached. "Good morning, Flossie. Have a good time last night?"

Flossie took a lingering look at Alecia's burgundy suit and gave a silly grin. "Lonnie Wayne is a lot of fun. He's one mean cowboy."

Not wanting to take the time to talk, Alecia went on to her room. As she stepped inside, a small figure jumped out from behind the door and yelled, "Boo!"

"J.D.! What're you doing back there? And you're at school early. Feeling better?"

"Lots better. Daddy had to go to a sale so he brought me early. I'm here to help you work. What can I do?"

Alecia looked into the soft brown eyes. "That's sweet of you and I appreciate the offer, but you need to be out playing with the other kids. It's a beautiful morning and the ball team needs you."

J.D. was disappointed, but undaunted. "I can help you quick, then go play." Her eyes darted about the room. "The erasers," she said, "I'll dust the erasers." Hurrying before Alecia could protest, she took the chalkboard erasers outside to slap them together, raising a white cloud in the fresh morning air.

Alecia set about readying her room when Lyle passed

37

her door. "Everything go all right at the Lassiters' yesterday?" he asked casually.

Alecia looked up from her work. "Yesterday? Oh, you mean taking J.D. home. No problem." She swallowed. Not much of a problem anyway.

"Good." He walked on.

J.D. returned the erasers and waited for a hug and a thank you before bounding out to play.

Alecia was the bell ringer today, since Flossie had playground duty. She watched the clock until it said exactly eighty-thirty, then stepped to the window to ring the old brass hand bell. She had the sensation of being caught in a time warp, as though her hair should be skewered in a high bun and her skirts sweeping the floor. Would it be so expensive to install an automatic bell system in the building? Before she could return to her desk, a commotion in the hall caused her to rush in that direction.

There in the foyer was J.D. sitting on top of a screaming, kicking Lanette, who was dressed in a ruffled blue sundress.

"Get off! Get off!" Lanette yelled in protest.

"Take it back!" J.D. answered with equal velocity. "Take back what you said, or I'll cream your ugly face."

"But you do," squealed Lanette. "You look like old Jake Shanks. You dress like him and his initials are J.D. Shanks. J.D.—just like yours!"

"J.D.!" Alecia spoke to her sternly. "Get off Lanette right now."

The child never budged. "Not till she takes it back. She's mean. I don't look like Jake."

"You do. You do." Lanette struggled to get loose of her opponent. "You never wear nice dresses."

"See Miss Winland?" J.D.'s eyes were dulled by the

inner hurt. "I'm gonna have to teach her a lesson."

"Not by fighting." Alecia stepped forward to physically lift her off Lanette's stomach. "Differences are never settled by fighting."

Noises from her classroom let her know the other children were taking advantage of her absence. Holding each girl by the shoulder, she steered them into the classroom and was surprised to see Lyle down the hall observing.

She swallowed the temptation to mouth an "I told you so." In her estimation, the trouble J.D. had experienced with Lanette was only the beginning. During recess, Alecia took the two girls aside and directed them to apologize to one another. But she couldn't shake the disturbed feeling she had about the matter. If only she were convinced that Rayne Lassiter's little girl really enjoyed dressing like a ranch hand.

Throughout the remainder of the week, Alecia kept close watch on the children to see if there were other underlying pressures against J.D. Nothing developed that she could actually put her finger on.

It wasn't until Friday that she remembered she and Nancy had plans for Saturday. She began to wonder what she would wear to a Field Day at an Agricultural Research Station. A stroll in Nicolett Mall it was not.

Nancy had said they would be outdoors most of the day, and yet she dreaded the thought of wearing the one pair of blue jeans she had purchased upon her arrival. It was Saturday morning before she finally decided on her wool slacks, a blouse, and a blazer for a jacket. Warm, comfortable, and sensible, she commended herself.

She was dressed and ready when Nancy knocked at her door. "Alecia, a letter from Mom and Dad," she exclaimed, obviously just back from the mailbox.

When Alecia opened the door, Nancy stopped and looked at her. "Are you sure you'll be comfortable in that all day today?"

"What do you mean? All my clothes are comfortable!" She turned and looked over her shoulder at her reflection in the mirror. "The cut disguises the bow in the legs quite well, don't you think."

Nancy chuckled. "Well, at least wear low-heeled shoes. Heels will never do."

"Hey, what do you think I am—a dude? I'll wear my boots!" In mock disdain, she snatched the letter from Nancy's fingers.

"Breakfast is almost ready." Nancy walked away shaking her head.

The tissuelike letter, postmarked Santiago, Chile, was light as a feather. Alecia marveled at her own parents, called out late in life like Abraham and Sarah, to the mission field.

Both Alecia and Nancy had been shocked when their parents announced they were selling the family furniture store in Nebraska to attend a two-year Bible college. Soon after graduation, they were applying for mission work.

Walt and Mattie Winland had been in Santiago barely three months when Nancy's surgery took place. Mattie flew home for a time and had offered to stay and help Nancy. But Alecia refused to allow it. "Mother, no," she said. "You go back to be with Daddy. I'll stay with Nancy."

"But you have your work, too, dear," her precious mother said, her eyes lined with tears. "It will be a sacrifice either way."

In the end, it was Alecia who flew back home, packed

her bags, and drove back to Oklahoma, and Mattie flew back to Santiago to work beside her husband.

Alecia sat in a chair by the window to scan the letter, full of news of the exciting, though tedious, work, and the difficulties they were having learning the language. "The children of our partners here," Mattie's neat handwriting read, "pick up the language so fast. It's not as easy for us old-timers."

Alecia smiled to herself. Before boarding the plane to leave the U.S. for the second time, Mattie told her daughter, "No sacrifice is without reward, Alecia. By releasing me to return to your father and the work there, you've opened the door for the Lord to work His perfect will in your life."

Perfect will? She stared out the window. There was no doubt in her mind God would work His perfect will. But when was she to know what that "will" was?

"Alecia," Nancy called from the kitchen. "This food is getting cold. Come on or we'll be late."

The Agricultural Research Station was larger and more complex than Alecia had imagined it to be. Hundreds of acres were under cultivation here, Nancy explained, with the sole objective of helping ranchers increase agricultural production.

When they arrived at the series of large stone buildings, the parking lot was already filled with pickups, jeeps, suburban vans, and a few cars. Instantly, Alecia recognized the Domiers' beige pickup and dreaded the thought that Lavren might be in the crowd.

The ranchers and their families had gathered in an area behind the station where a wide assortment of new farm machinery was assembled. Alecia wondered how much shin-deep grass she would have to drag her wool slacks through. As she and Nancy left the parking area, a familiar voice sounded behind them.

"Miss Winland!" J.D. came running toward her from where she had been playing with a group of other children and flung herself into Alecia's arms.

"J.D.! What are you doing here?" She returned her student's warm hug. She had seen the beige pickup, but had missed the royal blue one.

"Nancy, do you know J.D. Lassiter? J.D., this is my sister, Nancy Whitlow."

Nancy took the girl's extended hand and smiled. "I knew you when you were just tiny, but I've not seen you for a long time. You've grown up."

J.D. looked at her with smiling eyes. "Pleased to meet you." Turning her attention to Alecia, she explained, "Me and Daddy came to learn about the best pasture grass. We want to know how to make our steers really fat!" Her cheeks puffed out as she imitated the fat steer, then she giggled. She seemed pleased to be able to make both adults chuckle. Without warning, she called out to a group of ranchers standing near the building. "Daddy, my teacher's here!"

Alecia could feel her face growing warm as several people looked in their direction. Rayne emerged from the group and strode toward them. The contoured lines of his western shirt made his shoulders seem more broad. At his waist was an ornate leatherwork belt with a gleaming silver buckle engraved with the ranch brand. Alecia was pleased to see his eyes were smiling again. "Howdy, Miss Winland. Nancy."

Alecia wondered if Nancy detected her discomfort. Could he still be upset with her? He had used Nancy's first name, but she was, Miss Winland."

"Good morning, Rayne," Nancy greeted him. "Perfect weather for the Field Day."

"Perfect." To Alecia, he said, "How's your car been running?"

To her relief he was looking at her with the same openness she had seen when they first met. Even though she remained concerned for J.D.'s welfare, and more so since the fight with Lanette, it was clear she took the wrong approach. "The name's Alecia, remember? And the contrary car, it seems, acts up only when its owner takes a wild notion to step out of line."

"That a fact?" He beamed a smile at her. "Interesting car. If all the vehicles at El Crosse behaved like that, we might never get anywhere."

Alecia felt relief at his joke and felt he understood. She had been privately forgiven, even though Nancy stood nearby and J.D. bounced around them with boundless energies.

Rayne took J.D.'s hand. "See you ladies later," he said, touching his hat.

"What was that all about?" Nancy wanted to know as they strolled toward the demonstration area.

"Inside joke," Alecia said softly.

Grace and Neil Atwood greeted Alecia warmly, as did other neighboring ranchers who now recognized her, not as an outsider, but as one pitching in to help her ailing sister.

Nancy introduced Alecia to the Research Agronomist and the Plant Physiologist who were the Field Day Directors. Both men, two of five research scientists employed at the station, were personable and looked to be near Nancy's age. Alecia wondered how long they had toiled at the job of divulging their scientific knowledge to these strong-willed, hard-working ranchers.

Once the directors began demonstrating the farm machinery, Alecia forgot she planned to be bored. Newer items were demonstrated and explained in detail, as the men answered questions and comments from the crowd. The children played noisily on the fringes and teenaged boys stood with arms akimbo and in the same loose stance as their elders, watching with unconcealed interest.

Directly across the way, she saw Lavren Domier who stiffly nodded and smiled at her. Beside him stood his lovely wife in a stunning turquoise western suit with matching Stetson. Flaming curls lay carelessly about her shoulders. Corrine appeared restless, causing Alecia to presume she attended at the request of her husband—or orders, which might be more accurate. There appeared to be a sizable age difference between the two. Corrine couldn't be much older than Flossie, although a good deal more polished.

Alecia looked away from Lavren's glances, but she uneasily sensed them coming her way. Feigning indifference, she walked nearer a mammoth combine to be shielded from the stares. Within minutes she again felt the glances and looked up to see that he also had moved. This was crazy. With a ravishing wife like Corrine, why should he be staring at her? Still puzzled, she strained to give her attention to what Nancy was saying about a lift she needed for the larger-sized hay bales.

Following the machinery demonstrations, the crowd was directed to the field plots where the experimental pasture grasses were under cultivation.

J.D. stayed near her father, but at times turned to shoot Alecia a wide grin.

They were moving from the test strands of Weeping Lovegrass when suddenly Alecia felt Nancy clutch for her arm as she started to fall.

"Nancy. You okay?"

"I don't know. I feel lightheaded."

"We'd better get you home." Alecia was filled with relief for an excuse to get away from Lavren's gray eyes.

"No, no. I'll be all right. Help me get back to the main building. I'll sit down until we're ready for lunch and the ranch tour." She took a few unsteady steps. "I know I'll feel better after I rest. I always do."

Together they moved away from the test plots, with Alecia allowing Nancy to put her weight on her supportive arm.

It was cool and quiet in the deserted lobby of the Research Station. Alecia gently assisted Nancy to a comfortable overstuffed chair.

"Guess I still need to take it easy. Right?" There was exasperation in Nancy's voice.

"Right," Alecia agreed. "Sure you don't want to go home?"

"No, please. I'll be fine. I'm learning I need to rest periodically. Will you be a dear and run back out and take notes for me? They're going to be outlining the new fertilizer programs and if you take notes, I won't have to bother asking questions later."

Truthfully, Alecia wanted nothing more than to sit in the other chair opposite her sister and wait it out, but she couldn't refuse. "Got paper and pen?"

"In the glove compartment of the pickup."

Alecia stepped toward the door nearest the parking lot.

"Alecia?" Nancy called after her.

"Yes?"

"Thanks. You're such a blessing."

Alecia smiled. "Anytime."

Opening the pickup door, Alecia leaned in and rummaged through the glove compartment under wire cutters, pliers, and other tools, and found a small notepad and a pen. As she turned to go, she gasped as she found herself face to face with Lavren Domier.

"I didn't mean to startle you, Alecia," he said in a low honey-coated voice.

He had come up behind her like a preying animal. "You followed me! What do you want?"

The steely eyes held a glint of amusement. "Defensive, aren't you? What makes you think I want something? Is it wrong to be neighborly?" Two more purposeful steps brought him even closer. He held the edge of the door with one hand, and rested the other against the side of the cab, fencing her into a corner.

"Your sister doesn't seem to be feeling too well. She's not the tough old rancher she puts on to be, is she? You can see it's not healthy for her to be taking on such hard work. You need to encourage her to sell out and quit, Alecia."

Prickles of fear crawled up her back. "My sister makes her own decisions, Mr. Domier. I've never run her affairs and don't intend to begin now. Please step aside and let me get back. I've promised to take notes."

"Notes aren't going to do her any good if she's too weak to work. Like buying shoes for a man with no feet— senseless." His hand moved to her shoulder. Alecia cringed and her mind raced. Was it better to kick and slap, or scream and run? His hand slipped under her long hair and rubbed across her neck.

Without thinking, her hand flew up to knock his away.

As she did, she heard Rayne's voice from the back of the pickup.

"Domier," he commanded. "Leave her alone!"

Anger boiled red in Lavren's face as he drew back. Alecia rubbed her neck to erase the awful sensation of his touch.

"You okay?" Rayne asked.

Now that the incident was over, her knees turned to water. She nodded as she leaned against the pickup.

Though Rayne was taller, Lavren's stocky muscular form would have made it a close match if they went to blows. Alecia held her breath, praying it wouldn't come to that.

Presently, Lavren's anger gave way to a sinister smirk. "Well, well. My apologies, Lassiter. I had no idea the young lady was taken."

Alecia blushed at the connotation. Rayne, however, was unaffected. "Whether or not she's taken is none of your business. The point is, you seem to forget you are."

Lavren scowled. "Don't play nursemaid to me, Lassiter. Sticking your nose where it don't belong could get you in a whole bunch of trouble."

Rayne stepped closer, his voice low and easy. "Domier, you ought to know by now I don't scare easily."

"Some locos don't have sense enough to have a healthy fear," the older man countered.

Rayne had now positioned himself by Alecia's side. She felt him gently take her arm. "Then this loco is telling you to do your business dealings with other people. Leave Alecia alone."

A few moments of silence hung heavy as it became apparent Lavren was relenting—at least for the present. He glanced about as though it suddenly occurred to him their scene might have been witnessed.

The gray eyes came back to Alecia. "I'll be going, but I'd advise you to think about what I told you."

They watched as Lavren returned to his pickup rather than to the demonstrations. He honked the horn twice. When Corrine joined him, they left.

"Are you okay now?" Rayne asked again.

"Really, I'm fine." She shook her hair back and took a deep breath. "Thanks for the rescue. You and Sparkie make a great team."

"Nancy's sheltie?"

Alecia nodded as she moved to close the pickup door. "Sparkie was the one who chased Lavren off the last time."

"When was that?"

"One evening when I was checking fences in the south pasture. He came to tell me if Nancy's bull got into his heifers he'd kill it."

Rayne turned to face her. "The man's got a legitimate complaint. I'd be angry, too, if a polled Hereford bull got into my Santa Gertrudis heifers. It's just that Domier goes about things in the wrong way. Is Nancy planning to fix the fence or move that herd?"

"Jake Shanks is coming to fix it," she assured him, sensing the return of his show of cowboy arrogance. She stepped away from him. "We'd better get back. I promised to take notes for Nancy." Glancing at her watch she noticed she had been away for only a few minutes. The frightening incident had seemed to last for hours.

Nancy fared well with the afternoon tour. The ride in the tour bus from one ranch to the next gave her time to rest. Determinedly, Alecia put Lavren out of her mind as she surveyed the layout of the ranches. The individuality and complexity of each ranch fascinated her. Ranchers, by necessity, must be adept at several occupations, ranging from marketing and finance, to mechanics and construction, as well as the science of agriculture.

At the Atwood Ranch, Neil proudly stood by as his fourteen-year-old son, Kramer, explained how he had written, from scratch, a computer program of break-even cost analysis for his 30-head feeder calf operation.

Alecia's heart was pricked as she thought of the program she and Galen were developing in Minneapolis for gifted children to explore their talents as this young man had. What if Kramer lived in an inner city setting and had never touched a computer. He never would have known he could write a complete program. The Minneapolis project was vital, she told herself with new resolve. These and other opportunities must be made available to as many young people as possible.

Nancy must have been reading her thoughts. She leaned over and whispered, "Brainy, isn't he?"

Alecia smiled. "Sure is. Whoever said country kids were supposed to be klutzes?"

"Who, indeed?" Nancy said with a smile. And Alecia realized she held that misconception as much as anyone. They laughed together at the unspoken joke.

Nancy failed to mention that the barbecue supper was to be held at the El Crosse Ranch. By six o'clock, participants were back at the Research Station and from there drove their own vehicles to El Crosse for the evening. Alecia's assumption that she had seen only a fraction of the ranch was indeed correct.

The rambling, U-shaped home curved around a spacious courtyard that was covered with latticed beams interlaced with leafy ivy. Small trees grew luxuriously in open spaces of the courtyard floor, and trailing foliage from hanging planters gave the area a tropical atmosphere.

Josie barked orders in marine sergeant fashion to white-coated workers who were filling the long serving tables with delectable foods. Several men arrived early to help with the barbecue and the aroma filled the warm evening air. Josie recognized Alecia and greeted her with a modicum of friendliness. On the other hand, J.D. was ecstatic to have her teacher at her house again.

Alecia settled Nancy in a comfortable chaise, then strolled out away from the courtyard. She followed a series of stone steps down a small grade to where a swimming pool lay, still sporting its winter cover. Adjacent to the pool were lighted tennis courts that looked more inviting to Alecia than the pool. How many weeks had it been since she had played a rousing game with Galen? Much too long!

Rayne kept busy moving through the crowd, having switched his role from that of an observer to that of host for the evening. His fellow ranchers obviously respected Rayne and seemed to value his opinion in ranching matters. Alecia recalled Flossie's remark about Rayne keeping to himself. Quite the opposite appeared to be the case.

Presently, J.D. appeared through the shrubs at the edge of the pool. "Howdy, Miss Winland," she said. "You want to come see my room?" She pointed to a wing of the house with patio doors that opened onto the courtyard. "It's right up there."

"But J.D., the party's outside. It wouldn't be right for us to leave right in the middle of everything."

"It wouldn't?" she asked, brown eyes widening.

Alecia glanced back toward the courtyard and saw Rayne watching the two of them. She wondered what this father thought of J.D.'s attraction toward her teacher. Did he still think of her as meddling in his affairs? Actually, she was curious to see the girl's room.

J.D.'s mind was never quiet. She tugged at Alecia's hand. "Let's go ask Daddy if it's all right." Alecia could only follow.

The absence of Rayne's ever-present hat revealed softly styled dark hair. As they walked toward him, she marveled at the picture of confidence he presented. How could such an intelligent man be so mistaken about the one issue in his life that was nearest his heart—his own daughter?

"J.D.," he said to her gently as they approached, "all the other kids are playing hide-and-seek in the main barn."

Alecia caught the remark as a subtle hint for J.D. to stay away from this teacher.

"I know, Daddy," J.D. answered, bobbing on tiptoes in her excitement. "But can Miss Winland come see my room? Please? It'll only take a minute."

Rayne folded his long legs beneath him and sat back on his custom-made boots, to where J.D. could put her small arms around his neck. "That would be fine, sweetie, but Miss Winland's had a long day. She may just want to find a place to sit down and rest."

Now both sets of brown eyes were studying her. So he had lobbed the ball into her court, had he? Did he think she would just let it drop? "I am rather tired, J.D., but I'd like to see your room, too. So let's take a quick look, then I'll rest."

The girl released her daddy's neck and hopped up and down. "Goody, goody. See Daddy, she really wants to."

Rayne's reaction couldn't be measured since Josie came to him at that moment with questions about serving lines. Alecia did hope he wasn't angry with her again.

J.D. pulled at her hand, taking her to the main door at the center of the back of the house. They stepped into a paneled living room with an open-beam cathedral ceiling and a massive native-stone fireplace against the far wall. Above the fireplace hung a painting of cowhands clustered around an orange glowing campfire in snowy winter twilight. There was scant time to study the tasteful furniture arrangements as J.D. hurried her down the hall.

Alecia hoped against hope that she would walk into a room full of ruffles and lace, with stuffed animals and dolls galore. She wanted so much to be wrong about this whole thing. But her heart was crushed anew as they stepped into the room that was extremely neat and attractive, yet gave no hint that an eight-year-old girl lived there.

The furniture was dark walnut, firm and solid. The plaid bedspread and drapes were a mix of chocolate and pale blue. Fluffy rugs lay about on the russet carpeting, and the desk and dresser were neat and orderly. Nothing was really wrong with the room. Except for the obvious absence of cute and cuddly little-girl possessions. Not even a jewelry box on the low dresser.

"Do you like it?" J.D. asked insistently.

Alecia wanted to ask J.D. if she liked it. Perhaps she did. Perhaps she had chosen the colors. Perhaps she had no interest in dolls, doll clothes, doll houses, play dishes, and the like. Inwardly, Alecia once again asked the Lord to keep her from making hasty presumptions.

She looked down at J.D.'s expectant face. "This is a nice cozy room, J.D.," she said in carefully chosen words. "You're such a blessed little girl to live here."

The small face lit up in a smile. She turned to the dresser and brought a framed photo to where Alecia had seated herself on the bed. "Want to see a picture of my mommy?"

The photo showed two women standing in front of a two-story house graced in the entrance by large white columns. Alecia recognized one to be a younger Corrine Domier. The other woman, the deceased Mrs. Lassiter, was a bit more petite with darker hair.

"Your mother was very attractive. No wonder you're so pretty," Alecia told her.

"Aw," she scoffed. "I'm not pretty. You heard what Lanette and the other kids say. I look like old Jake."

"No, J.D. You look like your mother and you're very pretty." Alecia looked back at the photo. "Was your mother a close friend of Mrs. Domier?"

J.D. giggled. "I don't know about friends. . .they're sisters. That there's my Aunt Corrine."

Alecia let this morsel of information sink in. Jake's under-the-breath comment came back to her: "Those Lamison sisters used to be the nicest girls in the county." What did it mean? And the lovely Corrine, so feminine and talented. Why didn't she take an interest in her niece, the only child of her dead sister? Surely, she could add a mother's touch in this girl's life.

So Rayne Lassiter and Lavren Domier married sisters, which more or less explained the interrelationship she had sensed as they bantered back and forth that afternoon. It was a tangled, sticky web of circumstances of which she didn't care to be a part.

"Come on, J.D. That hungry mob will get in those lines and not leave us a crumb. We'd better get back."

J.D. replaced the photo on the dresser, pulled open the drapes, and let Alecia through the sliding glass doors that led back to the milling, laughing group of hungry ranchers.

Silently, Alecia made a vow that from now on until she left to go back to Minneapolis, she would strictly mind her

own business. Nancy may think Lavren was only a
blowhard, but personally, she didn't want to take any
chances with either Lavren Domier or Rayne Lassiter.

four

Kane Brake stepped gingerly, but proudly among the scrub oaks, making generous allowances for Alecia's novice riding abilities. The three of them—exuberant Sparkie included—searched out ravines and gullies, through heavy brush, for calving heifers or deserted calves that might starve to death without help.

The work was so appreciated by Nancy who was also delighted that her favorite horse was getting back into shape. Nancy's growing strength was allowing her to take on more housework and even the evening chores, but the doctor insisted she not be in the saddle too much or take bone-jarring cross-country trips in the pickup.

When Alecia volunteered to forego the pickup and use Kane Brake to scout the pastures, Nancy expressed surprise. Ironically, Alecia was as surprised as anyone. Never did she think she would volunteer to sit astride a mammoth animal and go gallivanting over the prairie.

Riding stable horses at summer camp was the extent of her equine expertise—and that dated back many years. But Kane Brake was a far cry from those old stable horses. This mare was highly sensitive with a distinctive personality all her own. Although her stance showed pride, her true nature was that of giving. . .humbling herself as she allowed this greenhorn to bounce awkwardly astride her back.

The month of April brushed the prairie with a palette of pastel wildflowers in lavenders and yellows. There was as much color now as there had been lack of it back in February.

A warm, flirtatious breeze ruffled Alecia's hair as she paused for a moment to watch a lingering sunset play a symphony of blazing pink and scarlet across the expanse of sky. Kane Brake waited patiently as Sparkie continued to sniff out every clump of tall grass about them.

Not since her childhood days at church camp, could she remember seeing such full, vivid sunsets. She recalled her favorite counselor, a girl of the ancient age of eighteen named Ruth. . .Ruth, like in the Old Testament.

Those lazy summer camp days drew her near to the Lord as she basked daily in the display of His handiwork. It was there in the woods near an open meadow, under Ruth's patient leading, that she made the decision to commit her life to God.

And even here, where the horizon stretched for miles, straight as the ocean's, with nothing but a few trees to block the majestic view, God seemed incredibly near. She enjoyed a ringside seat, with not one skyscraper to blot the brilliance of each new sunset.

Back at the stable, Kane Brake received a well-deserved brushing and grooming before Alecia finally returned to the house. Nancy called out from the den where she was resting. "Find anything?"

"I'm not as thorough as you or Jake," Alecia confessed. "I didn't ride down into those rough places in the northeast pasture, but in all other areas I found no bovines to rescue today." She placed her hat against her chest and bowed her head.

Nancy chuckled and waved her to a chair. "Good. We can relax then. Since gardening began and you decided to take Kane Brake out, I've missed our long evenings together."

"If I sat down for even a moment in that soft chair, I'd never get up. Let me shower, then I'll bring out my papers to grade. I wouldn't dare get the nods with a lapful of work."

In the shower, she purposely let the water run cool over her body to provide stimulation for another session of grading papers. In her heart, she only wanted to work on the latest material Galen had sent down from her office. She was beginning to doubt the wisdom of taking the position at Charlesy.

Stepping from the shower, she dried briskly, put on her nightgown, wrapped herself in a velvety robe, and scooped up the armload of papers. The ringing phone at her bedside pulled her back into the bedroom. "I got it," she called to Nancy before picking up.

"Hey there, prodigal child. Elusive runaway!" Alecia's heart tripped lightly at the sound of Galen's teasing voice on the other end. "If I'd known when I took this job that you were going to throw me to the lions and then skip the country, I'd have stayed back in Folwell Junior High trying to outguess the troublemakers."

Alecia giggled. "Galen, please. Have mercy. You're making me feel terrible." She propped herself up in the bed against the huge feather pillows.

"You noticed! Doesn't it make you want to rush back to Minneapolis right away?"

If he only knew, she thought. "What? And leave the lonesome little doggies to cry all alone in the canyons? You heartless cad. I knew when I met you there was something sinister in your bones and now I see what it is. Cruelty to dumb animals."

"You're the one who's cruel to a dumb animal—me!

This dumb animal was thrown into the midst of a press conference today without the known authority on the stepped-up Gifts and Talents Program that is due to be launched next fall."

"Oh, Galen," she sobered suddenly. "I didn't know Mr. Harwood was going to call one this early. How did it go?" Alecia knew Galen's heart was definitely in this project but he seemed to lack the ease and diplomacy that she commanded when working with the press and public. And he was the first to admit it.

"Those hard-nosed reporters bother me. I wish you had been here to melt their cold hearts and to act as my buffer." Tenderly, he added, "And I miss your warmth in my life as well. When are you coming back? Can't we hire your sister a herd of cowboys to get that work done so you can leave?"

Alecia missed Galen as well, but somehow she knew it wasn't quite the same with her. Just prior to Nancy's surgery, their relationship had taken a turn as Galen became increasingly serious.

"Good idea, Mr. Smartie," she bantered back at him, "but a herd of cowboys costs more than you or I could afford on our meager salaries. Besides, they're terrible at keeping up the laundry and dishes and such. And don't forget, I'm committed to the little school until May."

Galen groaned. "Alecia, how could you let yourself get into that bind?"

She chuckled. "I've been wondering the same thing. I guess it was most because of Nancy."

"I thought Nancy needed you there."

"She does, but she felt that I wasn't being stimulated intellectually and, when the opening came up, the school was desperate for a short-term fill-in. I was the logical candidate."

"So now you're stimulated intellectually by a room full of third- and fourth-graders, right?"

Alecia fanned through the stack of papers on the bed beside her. "How explicitly you word it, sir. But now, back to the press conference. What questions were asked? Were they fair?"

"Assistant Superintendent Harwood briefed me well. He and I went over all the possible questions early this morning and he had practically all my answers written out on cue cards. Embarrassing, but effective."

His humor buoyed her sagging spirits. "Galen, be serious."

"Well, well!" His voice lowered a pitch. "Just how serious do you want me to be?"

"Galen!" she spouted. He could be so exasperating, and so loveable.

"Okay, okay. For the most part, the natives were friendly. There were no surprises anyway. I'll send you the news clips as soon as they come out. You would have been proud of me."

Alecia smiled. She was more than proud of her working companion who had filled in for her and yet hadn't taken over her pet project. Consistently and continually, he forwarded memos and reports to her by the dozens. There was no way she could ever express how much she appreciated him.

She changed the subject then and told him about riding Kane Brake out over the rough terrain to search for new calves.

"You talk like you enjoy that kind of thing," he quipped.

"It's different."

"Well, my advice is don't get too attached to that

cowboy lifestyle." He paused and added, "Guess I should be thankful I don't have any competition other than a horse."

Cautiously, she avoided the seriousness of his comments and lamely joked her way into a goodbye. As she replaced the receiver, she wondered about their relationship. Had she not been in Oklahoma the past few weeks, would Galen have proposed to her by now? The thought frightened her. She was still unsure of her feelings. Galen's sensitivity was profound and he amazed her with the depth of his faith in God. But did that appreciation of him constitute love? A lasting love?

"Let me know for sure, Lord," she muttered as she headed for the den.

The next morning, she awakened to a radiant spring day. The birds in the hackberry trees outside her window were running the scales in efforts to touch the most exquisite notes. Her heart matched their songs. In less than a month and a half, she would be home again. Humming to herself, she pulled the jonquil yellow dress from the closet. This was her happy dress.

At school, she once again allowed J.D. to perform a small task in the classroom before scooting her out to be with the others. This had become a daily habit and she feared the other children would add "teacher's pet" to their list of teasing names for J.D.

The day was uneventful. At lunch, she had a reasonable conversation with Flossie that caused her to wonder if the girl had more intelligence than she let on. Perhaps her dumb female act was for the benefit of the men in her life.

Nancy had related to Alecia that Flossie had gone to college but instead of leaving home, she drove a distance of fifty miles each day for four years. Hardly the means of widening one's horizons in life, Alecia mused to herself.

At the sound of the bell that afternoon, students scurried out to pile on the bus but, within minutes, J.D. came running back in. "Daddy's not out there," she said. It was a declaration that didn't seem to disturb her.

"Just a minute, J.D.," Alecia told her. "We'll stop the bus and Mr. Jenkins can take you home."

"Oh no! Daddy'll be here in a minute, and if I'm on the bus, he'll miss me," she explained, eyes wide.

There were cleanup chores to be done in the room, then Alecia planned to drive to Kalado to pick up a few things at the store for Nancy before going home. She hoped they wouldn't have to wait long.

"That'll be fine, J.D. You can help by picking scraps of paper up off the floor while I separate these work sheets."

As they worked, Alecia found herself glancing at her watch every few minutes. What should she do if he didn't come?

She picked up scattered storybooks from the reading table and knelt down to slide them into the bottom shelf of the bookcase. As she did, she felt J.D. come from behind her to stroke her hair.

"Your long hair is so pretty, Miss Winland. Especially on your yellow dress."

"Thank you, J.D. I call this my happy dress because of the bright yellow color."

She felt small fingers go all the way down to the ends of the curls. Did this girl wish her hair were not cropped so ridiculously short? Whose idea was the haircut anyway? Could Rayne be so heartless? "Your hair is pretty, too, you know." Alecia turned around and ruffled the ringlets.

"Just look at all those curls God gave you. You're blessed."

Alecia started to rise, but J.D. just stood there close. "You're awful pretty, too," she said quietly. "I like you." Alecia looked at the intense pixie face. How this child must hunger for a mother's love. Josie was a loving soul, but Alecia couldn't picture the hard-working woman gathering J.D. in her arms and reading her a bedtime story.

"I like you too, honey. You're a special girl. Now," she said, clearing her throat and rising from her knees, "we need to make a decision. I need to drive to Kalado before going home. Can I take you out to the ranch?"

"I know Daddy will come by here." J.D. chewed her lower lip a minute as she thought. "How about if we leave him a note on the outside door? He can wait for us here and I can ride along with you." Her face brightened. "I love shopping."

Alecia nodded her agreement. "I'll be coming back by here on my way home so I guess it'll work. It's better than sitting here. Let's go."

The two of them talked and laughed all the way into town. At the grocery store, J.D. ran about, fetching items from Nancy's list and placing them in the basket. She was sure to bring only the sizes and brands that Alecia had named. Her unassuming attitude was endearing.

Alecia saw her eyeing the candy bars, but she asked for nothing. Before checking out, Alecia asked her if she would like one. She nodded and smiled her thanks.

As they walked to the car, Alecia once more remembered the dress in Archer's window. It wouldn't hurt to walk by and see if J.D. noticed it.

"Let's go window shopping for a minute, J.D. Sound good?"

"Sounds great!"

J.D.'s boots clomped along on the old brick sidewalk as they passed the donut shop and the insurance office on their way toward Archer's. It happened exactly as Alecia hoped it would. J.D. was pulling at her hand. "Look, Miss Winland. There's a happy yellow dress for little girls."

"So there is, J.D. Shall we go take a look?"

J.D. did a little skip, hop. "Oh could we?"

"Sure. Why not?"

She stopped. "Daddy may be waiting."

"You gave so much help in the store, we finished quickly," Alecia said. "And it'll only take a minute to look."

Convinced, J.D. led the way inside. Together they examined the rack of dresses in J.D.'s size. The girl oohed and aahed over each one, but kept going back to the yellow one like the one in the window. She touched the ruffled skirt and puffy sleeves as though it were fragile.

To think Rayne could afford to buy nice things for his daughter but refused to do so. It was cruelty at its worst. Alecia pulled the yellow one from the rack and put it up against J.D.'s slender body. "Want to try it on?"

"Really? Could I?" Her cheeks were aflame with excitement.

"I'd like to see you in it. The color would highlight the color of your hair."

In a few minutes, a transformed cowgirl burst out of the dressing room with a squeal of delight. Although it looked a bit strange with boots, the dress was otherwise lovely. J.D. twirled on her heel to make the skirt sweep out.

The salesladies smiled as they looked on. Impulsively, Alecia turned to one of them. "We'll take this one, please."

J.D. looked at her in disbelief. "But my birthday's not until summertime when it's hot, and Christmas is even farther away than that."

Alecia put her arm around the child. "Hasn't anyone ever given you a gift just because they cared about you?"

J.D. pondered the questions. "Daddy used to. . .a long time ago. Grandpa does, sometimes. He's neat." Then she thought of something else. "This dress is too pretty to wear to school. Where would I wear it?"

"Maybe you could go to church with Nancy and me some Sunday. Now, go change. We'd better hurry."

At the cash register, the saleslady boxed the dress. Looking over the counter at J.D., she said, "Aren't you Rayne Lassiter's little girl?"

"Uh huh," J.D. answered.

Alecia saw the woman shoot a strange sideways glance at the clerk beside her.

"And this," J.D. added, "is my teacher from Charlesy."

The lady handed Alecia her change and said, "You must be real new around here."

"I've been here since February."

The ladies exchanged glances once more. Alecia suddenly felt uncomfortable. "Hope you get a lot of wear out of this, little Miss Lassiter," the clerk said, handing J.D. the large box.

Alecia hurried J.D. out the door. Small towns, she fumed. Like living in a fish bowl. All she had done was buy the girl a gift.

As they approached the school, Alecia could see the blue pickup parked in front. Of course, Rayne might not understand at first, she assured herself. But once he saw how excited his daughter was and how cute she looked, there would be no way he could protest her having the dress.

She was wrong. Dead wrong.

J.D., box in arms, jumped from the car the moment it stopped "Look, Daddy!" she called out. "Miss Winland bought me a happy yellow dress. Wait till you see it."

Rayne stepped out of the pickup and approached them. The brown eyes were hard and resolute. "A dress, J.D.? What made Miss Winland think you needed any clothes?"

"We were waiting for you, Daddy. Miss Winland had to get groceries, so I went with her and we window shopped and I saw the dress and liked it and she let me try it on. Then she bought it for me because she loves me. Isn't that right, Miss Winland?"

In her very innocence, J.D. made the whole thing sound very contrived. Alecia felt her cheeks reddening.

"Where were you, Daddy? We waited a long, long time."

"Had a flat tire on the way back from a sale." His words came with no change in tone. "Give the dress back to Miss Winland, J.D. I'll buy your clothes for you. Go get in the pickup."

Taught to obey, J.D. looked at her father with an expression of stricken disappointment. Yet, without protest, she handed the box to her teacher with a, "Thank you anyway, Miss Winland," and walked slowly to the royal blue pickup and crawled up into it.

At the click of the door, Rayne spoke. "Archer's! Now all of Denlin County will be buzzing about the latest. Tell me, what gave you cause to think I can't buy anything and everything my daughter might need?"

"It wasn't because I didn't think you could."

"You didn't think I would. Is that it?"

"Rayne, please. It's just a gift. I'm fond of J.D. She's

a precious child. I wanted to show her my love with a gift."

"How about a coloring book and a large box of crayons?" His voice was laced with anger, his eyes flashing. "You don't want to give her a gift, Miss Winland. You want to crawl into her mind and rearrange her modes of thinking."

"There's no need to change a girl's way of thinking about a dress she loves." Her words came fast now, like bullets to the mark. "All little girls love dresses, Mr. Lassiter. Or haven't you noticed?"

"All I notice is a meddling, citified schoolteacher messing with my daughter's mind. Can't you people be satisfied with reading and writing? Think you got to psychoanalyze everybody? Let me tell you J.D. is a happy child. And if you keep meddling, I'll pull her out of Charlesy and drive her to Kalado to school."

Alecia shook her head in disbelief. If only he had seen his daughter dancing around the store in the frilly dress. But even then, he might not have accepted it. What had happened in his life to have blinded him so?

"It doesn't take psychoanalyzing a puppy to know it likes to be scratched behind the ears. Only a simple observation." The scalding accusation hung between them. "Very well," she said with sharp resignation. "I'll take back the dress. But I'll never be sorry I bought it." She whirled about and tossed the box in the back seat and jumped into her car.

This time, the car started immediately and provided the perfect opportunity to peel out and send a spray of gravel flying. Just in time, she remembered J.D. She couldn't make a scene in front of her.

She was far down the road before her ragged breathing began to even out. It had happened again. She had let her professionalism fall by the wayside and had allowed herself to be melted like warm butter by this precocious child—then ridiculed by her father. "Lord, what's happening to me?" she moaned as the wind whipped her hair and cleared her mind. Of all the children she had ever met, none had affected her like J.D.

What would have happened, she chided herself, if she had taken even one underprivileged inner city child to a dress shop for a new dress? If word ever got back to her superior, Mr. Harwood, he would have been extremely unhappy with her.

Oh why couldn't Rayne see the negative seeds he was planting in J.D. By the time she turned thirteen, the girl would be in rebellion for sure. Alecia turned the car sharply and the sacks slid across the back seat in protest. That would serve him right, she thought. Then he would see she had been right all along.

But was that really true? She recalled how J.D. respectfully handed over the box and obediently retreated to the pickup. It was the type of obedience Alecia had seen only in children with loving parental authority in the home. What a paradox.

Once before she had made a promise to the Lord—to hold both Lassiters at arm's length. Perhaps the only answer would be to resign her position at Charlesy before the year was completed. But the very thought that she would quit anything was repulsive to her.

Lost in her thoughts, Alecia drove past Jake's mobile home before she noticed him standing outside waving and grinning at her. Absently, she thrust an arm up to wave back as she rounded the bend.

She struggled to get her mind back into a semblance of order before talking with Nancy. Her sister had an uncanny way of sensing if anything was amiss.

five

"You sound just like Mother," Alecia told Nancy defensively. Her elder sister finally asked Alecia what was wrong. They were clearing away the dishes from supper. Alecia was struggling to mask her distraught emotions and, in doing so, had obviously become all the more transparent.

"I take that as a compliment," Nancy retorted good naturedly. "As Mother always quoted from Chapter Eight of Nehemiah, 'The joy of the Lord is your strength.' If so, you must be feeling pretty weak right now. You've uttered hardly two words since you came home."

Alecia thought back to her exuberance that morning as she donned the jonquil-colored dress. How foolish it was to let her joy ride on such an unpredictable yo-yo string.

"Oh, Nancy," she blurted out, thankful to be able to unload her misery, "it's the Lassiters."

"The Lassiters?" Nancy looked around from wiping down the cabinets. "What's the problem?"

"Come to my room. I have something to show you." In the bedroom, she retrieved Archer's dress box from her closet, opened it, and lay the dress across the bed. Against the flowered spread, the dress looked even more lovely.

Nancy sat down beside the dress, gently fingering a ruffle. "You bought this for J.D.?" Alecia listened for incrimination in the question, but detected none.

"I hadn't planned to. It just seemed to happen." How could she explain? "Rayne was late, so I took J.D.

shopping with me. We went by Archer's and she was crazy about this dress. I let her try it on, and she looked so darling and was so excited. . . ."

"And you just couldn't resist?"

"I know it sounds crazy."

"Does Rayne know?"

Alecia could only nod, remembering his anger afresh.

"What did he say?" Nancy's voice took on the sternness Alecia remembered from her childhood.

"He was terribly angry. He made J.D. give it back to me. Can you imagine? Poor child. She needs fussy things. You should have seen her in that dress, whirling and dancing."

Alecia sat down on the chintz chair by the window. "Why can't he see? He's hurting her unmercifully."

"You may be one hundred percent correct in your assumptions, Alecia. . .and I agree that you may be. But you're going about this all wrong. You're backing a wounded bull into a corner. No matter what you say or do, he's going to come out fighting. And this is a corner Rayne's never been in before."

Nancy folded the dress and placed it back into the box, tucking the rustling tissues around it. "Knowing Rayne," she went on, "I imagine it's a hard lump for him to swallow just to think J.D. has attached herself to an outsider. But for you to move in on his territory like this. Well, stop and think how you would feel if someone came into your office in the education center and began telling you how to run your business. Would you receive it, or resent it?"

Alecia leaned back in the chair, pondering Nancy's words. As usual, her sister was right. "I guess I owe him an apology, don't I?" A real one this time, she told herself. Not a subtle one.

Nancy smiled her approval. "Ever since Rayne's wife died, he's tried to shut out the world. But he loves J.D. deeply. Most of us who know him are trusting that in time he'll see clearly what his daughter needs most in her life. But he'll have to come to grips with it in his own way. That's just the way these people are."

Alecia puttered through the remainder of the evening, trying to keep her mind on her work. How would she ever find the opportunity to apologize to Rayne? And what good would it do anyway? He would certainly rebuff any attempts she made. Never would he believe she truly wanted to apologize with no strings attached.

By the time they settled down to their devotion time together, Alecia asked Nancy to pray that she would have the wisdom to handle the matter. However, even after Nancy's prayer, Alecia's frustrations were not eased.

By the time she readied herself for bed, she decided phoning was the only way. She lacked the courage to drive to the ranch and face him. But it had to be settled now. She paced the carpeted room for a few minutes, hands thrust deep into the pockets of her robe. Finally, she picked up the thin county phone book and ran her finger down the page listing to the El Crosse Ranch. Ever so slowly, she punched in the numbers.

"Come on, Alecia," she taunted herself beneath her breath. "You were brash enough spit at him like an old hen this afternoon; you can be bold enough to apologize like a woman now."

She dared not take a breath as the phone rang on the other end. A deep resonant voice answered. "El Crosse Ranch. Rayne speaking."

She froze.

"Hello? Who's there?"

"Rayne? It's Alecia."

A stretch of silence weighed heavyily. "Yes," he said finally, not unkindly.

"I called to apologize. Sincerely apologize."

"I see." Noncommittal.

"I guess I got carried away. J.D. looked so cute in that dress and kids always. . . ." She stopped. "Oh Rayne, the truth is, I don't know what got into me. I've been in the field of education for many years, and I've never been so drawn to a student before. It's crazy and I'm sorry. I'm not usually so impetuous. From now on, I promise to step back and become more objective about J.D."

Her heart pounded through another silence. Would he believe her? It mattered to her that he did, because now she was being totally honest. At least as honest as she could be. She really didn't know why she felt so strongly about the child.

"I'll give you credit," she heard him saying in his slow way. "It took courage for you to call."

"It was positively terrifying," she admitted.

"You didn't have to call."

"Yes, I did. We need to clear the air for J.D.'s sake. Believe me, I don't want to cause any anxiety for your daughter." She waited through another meaningful pause, only now the pounding of her heart had subsided somewhat.

"She's taken a real liking to you, Alecia," he said. "She doesn't usually buddy up to someone that fast."

Ah, good. Back to first names.

"And," he added with a touch of humor in his voice, "she's even giving the old multiplication tables a second glance now."

"That's music to a teacher's ears. To hear that a child

has become motivated to study."

"It's a real switch. Josie and I were having a rough time with her there for a while."

Alecia tried to envision Rayne sitting at the kitchen table like a normal parent, helping J.D. with her math. Somehow it just didn't fit. Absently, she wondered if he had his boots pulled off now, with his feet propped up on a footstool in the magnificent oak-paneled living room.

"Well?" she asked.

"What?"

"You haven't told me if you accept my apology after I've come forth in fear and trepidation to call."

"I do accept. And I appreciate the call."

She let these mellow words sink in, hoping he was sincere. It occurred to her that he might apologize to her for his anger as well. But after all, she hadn't called to bait him.

"Say," he added almost as an afterthought. "I've been wanting to ask. Have you heard from Lavren since the Field Day?"

"No. Why?"

"Just curious. Alecia?"

"Yes."

"If you do, you let me know. Y'hear?"

What is this? she wondered. They were talking about J.D. and homework, and all of a sudden Domier enters the conversation. She wanted to forget him forever. "For what it's worth, okay, I promise to let you know."

"Good. Thanks again for the call. You take it easy now. Bye."

Alecia felt strangely light and airy as she hung up the phone. Nancy was surely asleep by now, or she would be tempted to run in there and tell her sister how much better she felt about the entire situation. He had accepted her apology. As livid as he had been that afternoon, she never would have thought it possible. And if she hadn't talked it out with Nancy, the whole nasty incident might have continued to fester inside her for who knows how long.

Sweet, kind Nancy. Now that Alecia thought about it, her sister had seemed overly tired this evening and was showing signs of coming down with a cold. She made a mental note to call the doctor as soon as she got home the next day. No sense in taking chances.

It rained for the next three days. . .dreary, sodden, gray rain that lets not a pinch of sunshine squeeze through. The children were restless and Alecia reached deep into her storehouse of memories to come up with ideas to keep them busy during recesses. No sophisticated gymnasium equipment was available as there had been in Minneapolis where schools were prepared for weeks of bad weather.

One afternoon, Alecia was down on the floor helping the girls cut out paper dolls during the late recess. J.D. was sitting close to her and when they were alone for a moment, J.D. leaned over with scissors snipping and said in a low whisper, "Do you know what my real name is?"

"No, J.D., I don't. No one ever told me." It was true. Even on her school record there appeared only the vague initials.

"Want to know?" she asked.

"Oh, yes. Very much." She had often wondered what the initials stood for and why the name wasn't used, even at school.

"Joanna Darlene," she whispered with all the graveness of revealing a deep treasured secret. "J.D.'s just my nickname."

"I had a hunch it was," Alecia told her. "Would you believe when I was in third grade, the kids called me Allie for a nickname? I didn't like it because where I lived, the alleys were narrow streets behind the houses where everyone kept their garbage cans."

"Yuck." J.D. wrinkled up her nose. "Did you wish they would call you Alecia?"

"Many times."

"When we're alone," J.D. said, her face solemn, "without other kids around, would you sometimes use my real name?"

Alecia gazed at the gentle, trusting small face. She forced her mind to recall her most recent resolve—to back off and be objective with her. But how could she? And what would it hurt to promise this? There wouldn't be many more opportunities for them to be alone anyway.

"Okay, Joanna Darlene," she said, pronouncing each syllable quietly and with great care. "When we're alone, I'll use your real name."

Quickly, J.D. looked around, but no one had heard. She looked back at her teacher and smiled a thank you.

Alecia felt a rush of warm contentment flow through her.

Saturday was still gray and soggy. Nancy's cold had grown progressively worse. Since it had moved into her chest, the doctor suggested bed rest.

Alecia went out to check on the horses and the feeder calves, stacked wood on the back patio, and then went back inside. It was a perfect day to laze about and get caught up on back work.

Days like this made her miss her metropolitan lifestyle more than ever. If she were home, she would be at the spa today, swimming or playing a game of racquetball with Galen.

The rain chilled the spring air, so a fire in the woodburning stove was the answer to chase away the dampness. Soon, the fire was crackling and the coffee perking. On the card table in the den, she spread out the work Galen had sent her.

Carefully, she studied the charts telling which schools would be involved in the stepped-up program and the personnel involved. Her pen scratched out meticulous notes in a spiral notebook to share the next time Galen called.

Her longing to see Galen and her desire to return to her work seemed to bleed together in a vague blur. She was unable to fit her feelings in the proper cubbyholes of her mind.

Grabbing her coffee mug, she rose restlessly from her work to the bookshelves by the glass-fronted stove. From the shelf, she took down Galen's photo and studied the generous smiling lips that had touched hers so gently before she left him last winter. The squinting blue eyes that scolded her when she worked too hard and laughed at her when she lost a game of tennis to him. His fair blond hair was full, brushed back casually from his young, almost boyish face. She wondered if he had any such trouble sorting out his feelings for her. From the way he talked to her during their most recent phone conversation, she decided he did not.

When the phone rang, it startled her, nearly causing her to spill the hot coffee. She was thankful she had disconnected the extension in Nancy's room. She replaced Galen's photo and grabbed the phone. She was both surprised and disturbed to hear Lavren Domier's voice.

"Mrs. Whitlow?" he asked.

"This is her sister. Nancy's resting right now. What can I do for you?"

"Alecia!" he said dramatically. "So good to talk with you again, Alecia. I'm sure you won't mind giving Mrs. Whitlow my message. Please tell her for me that I have the bull. And that I meant just what I said."

Alecia bristled. "You're lying. Jake fixed that fence. He told me so. The bull couldn't get through."

"Alecia, dear. You women need to learn you can't trust a drunk. Maybe you'd better drive over here and see if I'm lying. I'd love to have you come and see me."

"If I come to your ranch, Mr. Domier, I'll have the sheriff with me. That bull belongs to Nancy. You can't kill him just because he broke through the fence."

"Bring the sheriff and his two deputies with him. We'll have a party," he said in his churlish manner. "But I must warn you, the law in Denlin County is more afraid of me than I am of them."

This man was talking crazy. Alecia had no idea how much to believe. "Exactly what is it you're wanting? You don't need Nancy's bull and I don't think you'd shoot him."

The calculating voice became even more so. "Don't kid yourself. I'd as soon shoot that bull as look at him."

"That's ridiculous. What would it gain you?"

"Well now, you're beginning to sound more interested. Drive over and we'll discuss the matter. You'll find me extremely businesslike in my dealings. After all, it wasn't my fault the bull came into my pasture."

His smugness was becoming more repulsive. "You seem to be forgetting, Mr. Domier, that bull is of no interest to me anyway."

"Please, not so formal. Call me Lavren. The bull, of course, may not interest you, but without that expensive bull, your sister's ranch would be in dire straits. I happen to know she's come on some hard times. And with your tender heart, you wouldn't want to see her lose the place. Right?"

He was right and he knew it. Ever since the evening he had approached her in the pasture, Alecia had been more concerned for Nancy's welfare. The simple solution seemed to be to sell and get out from under the pressures and hard work. But Alecia knew the love of this land was deeply ingrained in her sister's heart as much at it was in any rancher's in the county.

"What do you want me to do, Mr. Domier?" Never would she give him the satisfaction of addressing him on a first name basis.

"I told you. Come on over and let's sit down and have a long talk together. There are some things I feel you should be made aware of."

Alecia rubbed the back of her neck, remembering the sickening sensation of his touch. Perhaps he didn't have the bull at all and was playing cat-and-mouse with her. But for Nancy's sake, she felt she had to take the risk. "I'll be there in an hour," she told him.

He gave a low-throated chuckle. "Now you're talking. I'll be waiting."

Disgusted, she hung up without another word. Thoughtfully, she went to her bedroom and changed into her boots, blue jeans, and a warm shirt and jacket. As she sat on the edge of the bed to pull on her boots, she happened to notice the note pad where she had sketched as she talked to Rayne a few nights ago. Why hadn't she remembered sooner? He made her promise to call if she heard from Domier again.

Oh, praise God, she sighed. Rayne would help her.

Her fingers trembled slightly as she dialed and prayed that he would be there. She released her bottom lip from between her teeth when his voice came over the line. Briefly, she explained to him the gist of Lavren's call and his threats about the bull.

"And you told him you'd come over?" Rayne asked in a tone of disbelief.

She shrugged. "I didn't know what else to do."

"Stay put," he told her. "I'll be right over."

When she heard his pickup pull into the driveway a short time later, she met him out front to prevent waking Nancy. She felt it was wise to let her sister rest. Rayne would get this mess straightened out quickly.

Alecia wasn't certain if her heart sped up because of the circumstances surrounding the call or because of the way Rayne looked at her as he walked toward her. He touched his hat and gave a nod. His eyes were shining as they glanced over her outfit and returned to linger on her face. "A real dyed-in-the-wool cowgirl." His trim moustache outlined his smile. "You sure look different in that getup."

His attention was totally unexpected. Alecia firmed her hat on her head and returned his smile. "I'm ready to round up them mean cattle rustlers," she joked to alleviate her discomfort. She was delighted, however, that he seemed so relaxed. He had sounded concerned over the phone. Perhaps the situation wasn't so grave as she thought.

"Can you ride?" he asked.

She laughed lightly. "Due in part to Kane Brake's benevolent attitude toward me, I manage. Why?"

"It's too muddy to take the pickup, and I'd like to ride down and take a look at the south fence before talking to Domier. You game?"

"Why didn't I think of that?" she said. "I could have ridden down the fence line to see if he was lying or not. Roscoe could be calmly chewing his cud in his own pasture right now." As Rayne walked toward the stables, she fell into step beside him.

"Better you didn't," he told her. "Domier could have been down there waiting for you."

It upset Alecia to think Lavren could have set a trap for her, but more upsetting was the fact that Rayne should suspect him of doing so. And, she surmised, Rayne of all people should know.

They saddled the horses while making minimal conversation. Rayne allowed Alecia to take Kane Brake and he kindly accepted Peppy, muttering to the horse softly as he worked with her. Intermittently, he leaned down to pet Sparkie as the sheltie trotted in among them, appearing impatient to be off on this unknown mission.

The rain had subsided and a light mist veiled the air. Alecia appreciated the brim of her cowboy hat acting as a small umbrella to keep the moisture from her eyes.

They were several feet from it when they saw the break in the fence where Roscoe had plunged through. Rayne pointed it out silently.

"But I was so sure Jake had fixed it," Alecia protested. "He told me—"

"No doubt about Jake," Rayne assured her. "He wouldn't lie. He's a good old boy. Either he didn't fix it good enough, or somebody's been tampering."

Alecia's mind was unwilling to comprehend Rayne's innuendo. "I thought Lavren was leading me on. I was hoping he didn't have Roscoe at all."

Rayne turned in the saddle to look at her, his face soft through the opaque mist. "If Lavren Domier says he has something, he has it. And he's determined to use the incident to his fullest advantage."

"What are you going to do now?" she wanted to know.

His face lit up with a mischievous smile. "You mean, what're we going to do. You and I are going to get the bull back for Nancy."

"How?"

"Simple. We ride over and bring him home."

Everything in her wanted to protest, but he made it sound like they were stopping by the convenience store for a carton of milk.

"You've driven cattle, haven't you?" he asked, straightening in the saddle, sitting high and tall.

"Cows and calves. Not a bull." She remembered Roscoe's mammoth size. He was a giant.

"No different." As though that settled the issue, he urged Peppy down to the fence and let her step neatly over the limp strands. Kane Brake followed as though Rayne were in control rather than Alecia. "Sparkie and the horses will do all the work," he said over his shoulder. "Come on."

He put the cow pony into a smooth canter and again, Kane Brake did the same. Alecia decided to relax and enjoy the loping ride. It seemed strange to think of the two of them coming across the back part of Domier Ranch and Alecia had no idea what they would do when they arrived at the feed lots.

But Rayne had everything all figured out. Since it was a rainy Saturday, he told her, most of the ranch hands would be inside the bunkhouses.

Cresting a small rise, they reined in their mounts to look for a moment across the Domier spread. The expanse of the ranch was larger and more complex than that of El

Crosse. Alecia scanned the multiple pens of feeder cattle, the large silos, and myriads of smaller buildings set about. The stately two-story white home of Lavren and Corrine Domier was on the far side, facing the road, graced about by towering shade trees, all gleaming fresh and clean after the rain bath.

At rare intervals, the sun found peepholes in the slate gray skies, forcing bright beams to lay golden patterns on the washed earth. The damp pasture gave off sweet fragrances. Appreciatively, Alecia sucked in the delicious aroma with a deep breath.

She turned to catch Rayne studying her. Embarrassed, she turned her eyes back to the pens below them. Her face felt warm beneath his gaze. "We'll never find him in all those feed lots," she said absently. Was he still trying to figure her out? Is that why he was watching her? Still not trusting her?

Rayne dismounted and called Sparkie to him. "We have our bloodhound with us," he explained. The sheltie's alert black eyes glowed in readiness. Rayne rubbed the thick fur. "Roscoe, Sparkie. Find Roscoe for us. And no barking either. You hear me?"

Alecia was surprised that Sparkie was so quick to obey Rayne. But the tall rancher seemed to have a way with all animals. She wanted to laugh at the thought of Lavren Domier sitting in his big white house, waiting for her to arrive, while she and Rayne were taking the bull out the back way. Sparkie sniffed out the bull in short order, locating him alone in a catch pen near where they rode in. It was a simple matter to open the gate and let Sparkie deftly run him out.

The mammoth bull seemed relieved to be released from captivity and was more than happy to comply. In a matter of minutes, Roscoe had lumbered over the break in the fence and was safe again on Whitlow land.

The gray clouds above them were beginning to thicken again and move in low. Rayne pulled Peppy to a halt. "We should put Roscoe in another pasture, just for good measure," he told her. "I'll send Sammy and a couple of the boys over to fix the fence later. We'll leave it up to Nancy whether to leave Roscoe there and run the cows in there with him, or put him back here and trust it won't happen again."

"I thought," Alecia said, as they rode across the muddy pasture with Roscoe and Sparkie in the lead, "it might be best that Nancy didn't know about all this."

"I understand you're wanting to protect her, but she'll have to know. She has to be on top of all that goes on here. It's the only way to run a ranch—recuperating from surgery or not." He glanced at the clouds that were churning with mounting fury. "We'd better hurry before the bottom falls out of that."

The convulsing, yellowish clouds brought to Alecia's mind all of the Oklahoma tornado stories she had heard. The first of the fat drops struck them as Rayne closed the gate after the bull. Vicious stabs of yellow lightning ripped through the clouds and explosions of thunder shook the ground. Both horses nickered nervously.

Rayne came up behind her, talking softly to Peppy, calming the old cow pony. "Mind getting wet?" His expression was almost like an apology.

She laughed, pulling her hat down more snugly over her eyes. "Wouldn't matter much if I did. I never learned to stay between the drops."

His laughter joined with her. "Lets head for the house then." The horses galloped neck-and-neck out across the great expanses of openness. They were nearly to the gate that led to the stables. The horses were clamoring up out of a steep draw. The rain was pelting them unmercifully. Alecia remembered thinking what a shame it was that Rayne's leather coat should be getting wet. At that moment, Peppy—surefooted Peppy—stepped into wet clay and went down.

Rayne's lean muscular body was at once alert and, like a graceful agile cat, leaped out of the way before being pinned beneath the horse.

Alecia stifled the scream in her throat.

six

To see Peppy go down, to hear her cry of fright also terrified the normally placid Kane Brake. Alecia fought to hold her in rein.

"Whoa, girl. Settle down. Easy now." She kept her voice steady, speaking between throbs of furious thunder.

Peppy jumped to her feet quickly, seemingly unharmed, but with a wild glare in her eyes. One more clap of thunder could send the frightened animal off on a dead run, only to be hurt worse.

Rayne stepped toward the pony to grab hold of the dragging leather straps but Peppy backed up, whinnying in fear. As Peppy moved backward in her direction, Alecia gently urged her mount forward.

Kane Brake was unsure, hesitant. Using all her strength, Alecia held tight, urging, encouraging. "Come on, girl. Move up there. Don't be afraid. That's a good girl," she cooed repeatedly.

Peppy regarded them with wide eyes as they approached and was somewhat calmed to see that Kane Brake was still there. Gradually, Alecia moved Kane Brake close enough so she could reach for Peppy's bridle. As she did, Rayne ran to them, retrieving the reins and quickly checking the horse's legs for possible injuries.

"Looks okay," he called out over the noise of the storm. "But no sense in taking any chances. I'd better ride back with you."

She held Kane Brake in check as he swung up behind

her. Immediately, she was aware of him as he reached around her to take the reins, his arms pressing against her shoulders. Rayne emitted an essence of tender strength that was measured not simply in physique, but in the very core of his personality.

Together they rode, leading Peppy back to warmth and safety. The dampness of the spring storm hung heavy in the stables, intensifying the aromas of leather, wet horses, and sweet hay. It was a relief to leave behind the blustery elements, which continued to beat against the metal building as though in a vain, but persistent, effort to get at them.

"Good piece of riding there, Calamity Jane," Rayne said as he dismounted.

"You didn't give too bad a performance yourself, Mr. Hickok," she countered. Outwardly, she threw off the compliment, but inwardly she savored it. She swung her leg over to slide down. Rayne reached up to assist her. "What say we take the act cross-country? A world wide event," she said.

She landed on the ground before him, but his hands stayed about her waist. He laughed aloud. "Training for that performance would be sheer agony."

She enjoyed the sound of his deep laughter. Laughter that played its own gay melody inside her.

"There's more power in your small arms than a fellow would guess," he said, still not releasing her.

"Tennis arms," she retorted. There were flecks of mud splatters on his cheek. Instinctively, she reached up to wipe them away.

"I play tennis, too," he said, his tone going soft. His hands slipped from her waist around to her back, enfolding her to him.

She heart beat against her chest as she looked up into his searching eyes that were nearly black in the dim, storm-darkened stable.

He lowered his face to hers. "We'll have to play sometime." The very breath of his words lay on her lips.

It was so natural, so easy to rise on tiptoe to meet the warm lips and return his embrace. Her hat fell silently to the stable floor. Her hands moved up his wet jacket to cling to his broad shoulders.

His kisses moved to her rain-streaked face, to her eyelids, and back to her mouth where she felt an inner explosion that equaled the rolling thunder shaking the vast prairies about them.

Already breathless from the ride, they were now weak and breathless from the storm of emotions rising between them.

She moved to touch his face. When she did, he took her hand firmly, then the other one, and stepped back. The brown eyes were smoky, troubled.

"Go on in and change, Alecia," he said evenly. "Before you catch cold. I'll tend to the horses."

Her mind and senses were reeling. She feared if he released her hands, she would surely fall. She nodded her mute agreement, struggling to control her thoughts. She pulled her hands from his and shivered. She was chilled.

Rayne watched as her lithe form bent down to retrieve her hat and place it firmly on her head before going out the door to return to the house.

Whirling around, he blindly slammed his fist into the support post of the stable, shaking it from top to bottom. Then his towering body sagged against it, as he leaned there, letting his anguish consume him.

Never, he vowed to himself, would he be so foolish as

to let uncurbed emotions deceive him again.

For the next few days in the classroom, Alecia could not bear to look into Joanna's eyes, because of the disturbance within her of seeing Rayne's eyes reflected there. They were so similar in expression and beauty. Ironically, the more she tried to evade the child, the more Joanna clung to her.

Endlessly, Alecia's mind replayed the moment when she slid off Kane Brake into Rayne's arms and into a bottomless abyss of stirred feelings.

And why? Why had he kissed her? She thought he detested her. Confused, she grappled with elusive questions. If he cared for her at all, why wouldn't he listen to her suggestions regarding Joanna? Perhaps there was no caring at all. . .just a lonely widower starved for affection. Had the embrace been an impulse at a weak moment? She threw out that possibility. One thing was certain, Rayne Lassiter was not impulsive.

Nancy had graciously thanked both of them for their help in bringing Roscoe home and eagerly accepted Rayne's offer to send men to repair the fence. Like the coward she was, Alecia chose to stay in her room while Rayne came in to call Lavren. Nancy told her later that the two men exchanged heated words over the phone. But Alecia made a pretense of taking more time than was needed to change, timing it to finish just as he left. There was no way she could face him at that moment—in front of Nancy.

Lavren's actions had not upset Nancy in the least. "Lavren's not actually ruthless," she explained to Alecia. "But he's had his eyes on my ponds for quite some time. He figures he can needle me into selling now that I'm having a rough go of it. Plus there are other problems he's struggling with."

Alecia was indignant. "Ponds? He has ponds. I saw them."

"The Whitlow land has two spring-fed ponds, Alecia. A lovely miracle of God. No pumping water ever. That's why Ted purchased this land in the first place." Then Nancy added with the old fire returning to her tired eyes, "And when I do let this land go, it won't go to Lavren Domier! I can tell you that for sure!"

Alecia moved slowly about her classroom as she remembered their conversation. No matter what Nancy said about Lavren not being ruthless, Alecia wasn't totally convinced. And she didn't see how Nancy would have the strength to go on fighting against him.

The schoolroom windows were open wide, letting long-awaited April sunshine splash into the room. It beckoned to the children to come outside, making them restless at their work.

When Alecia first arrived to teach at Charlesy, her students roamed about the room at will and talked continually without permission. But through perseverance and by using a rewards system, she soon had them striving to earn credit points by obeying the rules she established. When there were enough overall points between the two grade levels, she rewarded them with Friday afternoon parties. This promoted team efforts and encouraged all students, rather than just a few, to participate in the system.

At first, they groaned and complained under her leadership, but gradually their allegiance came around. She rejoiced to see them begin to strive for academic excellence.

Although the days were warmer and sunnier than ever,

Joanna dallied behind in the classroom at every recess—except when Alecia had playground duty. It became a source of worry for Alecia. Now, more than ever, she realized she should never have purchased the little yellow dress. In doing so, she had unwittingly cemented their relationship.

By the time the afternoon recess rolled around, Alecia made up her mind about something. Asking Flossie to take over for her on the playground, she hurried to Lyle's office and knocked lightly at his door. His small office was situated just off the fifth- and sixth-grade classroom.

He invited her in without getting up from his ancient wooden swivel chair situated behind the desk. She stepped in and he gestured toward the only other chair, which had a torn vinyl seat.

"What's on your mind, Miss Winland?" he asked, smoothing his hands across his thinning hair.

"It's J.D.," she said, scooting the chair closer to his desk. She had to be careful not to use the lovely name of Joanna.

Lyle raised craggy eyebrows, but said nothing.

"She's become very attached to me and I want to resign now before further damage is done in her life."

There. It was finished. She let out a sigh. If all went well, she could be back at her desk in the Minneapolis Educational Service Center Office within two weeks. She was sure Nancy could get along fine now. Suddenly, she felt exhilarated.

Lyle studied objects on his desk for a few moments, then leaned back, folding his hands behind his head. "I'd sure hate to see you quit now, Miss Winland. For several reasons."

"I realize it could leave you in a bind, but surely you can get a good substitute for the few remaining weeks." She took a long breath. "I was wrong to try to become involved in J.D.'s personal life. I can see that now." In her mind's eye, she was already packing.

Lyle's hands came back down and were folded on the desk top before him. The old chair creaked in protest. "Miss Winland," he said, "I've observed with mounting interest the transformation in your students since you've come here. And I want you to know it's a joy to me."

She started to speak, but he raised a hand to stop her. "Flossie also watches you like a hawk. She's young and impressionable." Lyle's eyes, which Alecia normally thought to be a bit dull, held a new spark. "In times past," he continued in his quiet manner, "I have approached our school board with new ideas, and have been repeatedly rebuffed because of lack of understanding on their part. But you've sort of slipped in the back door, so to speak, and introduced innovations, simply by your presence, that I couldn't have done in my position."

Alecia shifted in the uncomfortable chair and fingered the fringed belt of her dress. This conversation was taking an unexpected turn, throwing her off track.

"On our small operating budget, there's no way Charlesy School could afford someone with your caliber of expertise, but here you are right in our midst. I've looked upon your being here as sort of a little miracle." Embarrassed by his own admission, he scooted back the chair with a clatter and rose to fetch a cup of coffee from the pot on the filing cabinet, which Mrs. Turner perpetually kept perked for him. He filled his mug and waved the pot at her, raising his brows in question.

"Yes. Black, please." Where was this strange conversation leading?

He brought the steaming cups and reseated himself. "It

has been," he went on with fresh composure, "a continual challenge here to discover methods to interest children in academics. To see your students' enthusiasm with their science projects and their spelling contests was a surprise to Flossie." He gave a wide smile. "And I'd almost forgotten how much fun kids could have in the process of learning."

"I appreciate the kind remarks," she said feebly. She never thought that by doing the things that were natural for her, that she was making a contribution. On the contrary, she felt like she was rubbing against the grain.

"Because of your being here, I had planned to undertake an all-school drama," he continued. "This would be an effort to initiate more parental involvement. I was going to present it to you and Flossie today after school." He rummaged in his desk drawer and pulled out a play script copy and handed it across the desk to her. "This is a patriotic analogy, which is both educational and entertaining."

Alecia flipped through the pages with growing interest. She could envision the sixth-grade boys excitedly building stage sets and painting scenery. "Looks like an excellent story line," she commented, scanning the pages. "It's a good script. If they've not been involved in much drama, they'll love doing this."

"Until now," he confessed, "I haven't had anyone who could take the ball and run with it. I know you can. You can arrange for tryouts and plan a fair way of casting, plus choose teams for the supportive work so every student is involved."

She nodded. She could at that. And interestingly enough, she felt a genuine desire to try.

Lyle's eyes narrowed as he watched her. "Just a few

more weeks? Charlesy needs what you have to offer."

Alecia thought about Davey, the boy who had been tough and swaggering when she arrived. At his young age, he already had the idea that enjoying school work was beneath his macho image. But he launched into a science project in entomology that astounded his classmates. But still, there remained the problem of Joanna Darlene Lassiter.

As though perceiving her thoughts, Lyle added, "I know I initially objected to your involvement in J.D.'s life, but I've also seen changes for the good in her. I know you feel she is dangerously close to you, but is any relationship without risk?"

This was a new side of this man she was now observing. It shamed her that she had underestimated his depth of perception.

"Even if J.D. never saw you again, you've taught her to be aware of new concepts and feelings she never knew existed."

As indeed, her father has done to me, Alecia thought ruefully. Was it really because of Joanna, or was it because of Rayne that she had suddenly decided to break and run? Discernment eluded her at this point. It was just too painful to sort out.

"The younger Lassiter," Lyle continued, oblivious of her thoughts, "is now aware there is more to this old world than branding cattle. What do you think? Will you stay?"

Well, she thought with a long sigh, so much for being back home in two weeks. She took the script. "When do you want to hold tryouts and when is the drama scheduled?"

Lyle drained the last of his coffee that was much too strong for Alecia's taste. "Tryouts, in three days; presentation, the night before the last day of school."

"Sounds fine." She stood to her feet. "I'd better go. Recess is nearly over."

Her boss pushed back the creaking chair and came around the desk to extend his large hand. "I don't think you'll be sorry for staying. And I'm very grateful. Really."

Before the day was out, Alecia had outlined plans to incite the interest of every student and devised costumes that would be quick and simple to make.

She wondered how Flossie would accept her as the director of the show and was pleasantly surprised to note that her coworker's enthusiasm was as high as that of the children's.

When the two of them met together before and after school to line out details, it opened a new door of acquaintance. Alecia discovered a not-so-dumb girl dwelling behind a barrier of low self-esteem. Cautiously, kindly, Alecia searched for ways to draw out Flossie's talents and abilities.

She invited Mrs. Turner and Mrs. Dominique to assist in voting for those who tried out for parts. She wanted to make it as fair as possible. Also, she realized that those who were voting were aware of Joanna's background and would refrain from giving her a part.

"If you don't get a part," Alecia explained to Joanna in an attempt to prepare her for the inevitable, "I want you to use your artistic talents to be costume designer with me."

"Thanks, Miss Winland," she said, "but I'm going to be Betsy Ross. I'm going to be the best one in the play. Then they won't say I look like Jake Shanks."

Alecia was sure that after Joanna became involved with the costumes, she would be just as contented as if she had a play part.

Noisy and excited, the children gathered in the gymnasium the afternoon of the tryouts. Flossie was seated beside Alecia on the front row of folding chairs that had been set up in the gym. She tucked a strand of hair behind her ear. "This is the most fun I've had since I started teaching," she quipped.

Alecia studied the face that could have been more attractive if the hair were shorter and softly fluffed to minimize the sharp angular lines. "I'm so glad," she answered. And she meant it.

"Hey, you know what?"

"What?" Alecia shuffled through the sheaf of papers in her clipboard.

"I've accepted a job in Ponca City for next fall. I'm renting an apartment up there and everything."

Alecia was astonished. "You're leaving Charlesy?" The girl who hadn't even left home to go to college?

"Lonnie Wayne isn't too happy about it, but I don't care. Mama says he's not very good for me and I guess she's pretty much right." She flipped through the script book on her lap. "You know," she said slowly, "I didn't much like you when you first came here."

And how I knew it, Alecia thought. But she appreciated the honesty.

"But now I think you're okay. All the kids like you and you make me want to be a better teacher." Flossie blinked her pale eyes that were dabbed with a hasty touch of eye shadow. "I want to learn to motivate kids like you do. I want to do more with my life and I don't think I can do that here." The last comment hung in the air like a question.

"Go for it, Flossie. You can be anything you set your mind to be. Your only limitations are in your own mind." She patted the girl's thin shoulder covered by another wild tee shirt. "I'll be praying for you to make the right decisions in your life. Now," she said, rising to address the Charlesy student body, "we'd better get this show on the road."

At home that evening, Alecia reviewed the results of the tryouts and was mortified to see that all the staff, except her, had voted for Joanna to play the part of Betsy Ross. She wrestled with the predicament. What would Rayne say if his daughter were dressed in a costume for a play? Would that be different than a yellow dress from Archer's?

At least Alecia would stand guiltless since this was none of her doing. The child had received the part, fair and square.

When Joanna stepped on that stage during the tryouts, she displayed none of the giggly nervousness of the other students. Her voice was clear and unwavering: "You're asking me to sew the first flag for our infant nation, General Washington? Oh, that I had a thousand hands to set to the task of such a noble purpose." Dramatically, she clasped her hands over her heart. "I am indeed humbly grateful to be chosen."

As indeed little Joanna would be humbly grateful when she learned she snagged the part.

Before Alecia was able to sit down to her school work that evening, it was quite late. The warmer the weather grew, the more work there was to do around the ranch. The pace that once seemed painstakingly slow, was now accelerated. Never was there lack of something to do.

And Jake was there nearly every day, often sitting down to supper with them, always entertaining them with stories of happier times in his life.

Once, Alecia asked Nancy why she kept him on since he

had such a drinking problem. "He's all I can afford," her sister answered with a shrug. But Alecia felt it was because Nancy was the only person who would extend to the man the gesture of trust and acceptance.

On this particular evening, Nancy had offered to clean up after supper so Alecia could get to grading her papers. But learning the results of the tryouts troubled and distracted her. She was curious what Nancy might have to say about it. Her sensible sister might tell her to pull the child out of the whole mess immediately.

To her surprise, Nancy seemed quite pleased with the idea. "A play part, you say? Betsy Ross?" She wrung out the dishcloth and spread it on the towel rack by the sink. "Sounds charming."

"But what about Rayne?"

Nancy grabbed a jar of hand cream and smoothed fragrant cream into her chapped, work-worn hands. "What about him?"

Alecia felt miffed. "Have you forgotten all of what you said to me about intrinsic pride, ingrained sense of survival, and all that propaganda?"

Nancy chuckled gaily. "I told you those things when you were on the man's case with all the stops pulled out. This is different. If, as you say, she was chosen by several voting adults, then I hardly think Rayne would object. This could be a foretaste for him of things to come. Oh, and by the way," she went on, totally changing the subject, "Corrine called me today."

"Domier?" Alecia couldn't imagine Corrine picking up the phone to call Nancy. They were total opposites. Corrine spent all her time training her prize horses and traveling from show to show, dressed to the hilt in western suits of every hue of the rainbow.

"Of course, Domier. She calls me every once in a while when she has exciting news. She's back from Texas where she won first place in one of her more important shows in the Western Pleasure Futurity Division. She called to invite me to the party Lavren is letting her give next Saturday night to celebrate."

Alecia's ears caught the word, letting. Obviously, the mistress of Domier Ranch could do little without Lavren's permission. It was a wonder he let her show the horses at all, strange fellow that he was. Alecia had not seen him since his anger simmered at her and Rayne for getting Roscoe back. When Rayne's men repaired the fence, it must have knocked some of the wind out of his sails. Alecia was thankful the invitation was for Nancy. She had no intention of going near the man ever again.

But just as though it were all settled, Nancy added, "The invitation was extended to both of us, and Corrine will be sending an escort for us."

"That's nice of her, but I can't possibly go," Alecia protested a little too quickly. "With the play and all, there's already too much to do."

"Nonsense!" Nancy waved her hand, still shiny from the cream coated on it. "Too much work and no play, you know. Besides, I've not been able to entertain you at all since you've been here." Alecia noted a hint of disappointment in her voice. "Had you come under better circumstances, we would have had so many opportunities for good times."

In her haste, Alecia had failed to consider Nancy's feelings in the matter. Of course she would have to go. If she refused, in all probability, Nancy would refuse as well. She shivered as she thought of Lavren. Surely the sour man would keep his distance at a celebration party.

Alecia wondered how Nancy could hobnob with the Domiers on a social level after Lavren had been so cruel to her. And from what Jake had confided to her, there were other instances in the past when Mr. Domier made life difficult for Nancy.

But Nancy remained undaunted. Whenever the subject of Lavren came up, she would say, "I just pray for him. He has no defense against my prayers."

Alecia knew she, too, needed to pray, not only for Lavren, but for herself—that she might forgive him for his advances toward her. She knew it was dangerous to let bitterness fester.

Since it was Alecia's first opportunity in months to attend a dress-up event, by the time Saturday arrived, she was determined she would make the most of it. She treated herself to a luxurious soaking in the tub amidst mountains of fragrant bubbles. She hadn't realized just how much she missed dressing up for evenings out with Galen to the theatre, a concert, or one of their special downtown, midnight suppers together.

Deciding what to wear, wasn't difficult as she had brought only one formal dress—and marveled that she even thought to pack it. She took ample time with her makeup, applying dark mascara to the very tips of her long lashes and color to her lips and cheeks. Not because of the occasion, but for the sheer joy of fussing with her appearance once again. Never had her complexion appeared so radiant and alive. Surely, there was something to be said for fresh air and sunshine.

Her chestnut curls, she decided, would be piled casually atop her head. Smiling at her reflection, she wondered if Lavren Domier would send one of his cowhands in a muddied ranch truck to fetch them.

Nancy interpreted Alecia's fussing to mean she was excited to attend the party, and Alecia hadn't the heart to tell her otherwise. Actually, she would rather be going anywhere than to the Domier home.

Nancy was attractive in her floor-length jade dress, but it concerned Alecia that not even the dress and makeup could mask the tiredness in Nancy's eyes. She wished she could convince the determined ranch lady not to work so hard.

The door chimes sent Alecia hurrying through the front hall, brimming with curiosity to see their escort.

Her very heart melted to see Rayne standing there.

seven

Rayne's presence filled the doorway. He was taller, more handsome than ever in his gun-metal blue suit. "Hello," he said casually, as though he dropped by every day of the week. "Corrine told me you all were coming to her little shindig, so I offered to come by. Hope you don't mind."

Other than fleeting glimpses of Rayne in his pickup at the school, she had not seen him since the rainy day in the stables. Now, as she looked up at the wide gentle eyes, the square jaw line, the full lips, her memories of that day grew warm and glowed inside her like hidden coals in the gray ashes of a woodburning stove.

Instantly, she caught herself, for fear he could read it in her eyes. "Mind? Heavens, no." She stepped back from the doorway. "Come in. Nancy's nearly ready."

It never occurred to her that Rayne might attend this affair. Especially after the strong words he had had with Lavren at the Research Center and the even stronger words on the phone following Roscoe's rescue. But, after all, Corrine was his sister-in-law. Perhaps that had some bearing on the situation.

She led him into Nancy's formal living room. "Been catching any cattle rustlers lately?" she asked glibly, waving him to the flowered love seat. It made her almost angry to think he could now fraternize with Domier after the awful things the man had done. And to think he could just walk in here like nothing had happened between her and him that rainy day. Did this man have ice water in his veins?

"No time," came the succinct reply as he sat down. "Too busy with calving and spring roundup."

"Catch 'em red-handed, then hobnob with 'em at the area's social gatherings," she remarked. "Is this some unwritten 'live and let live' code of the old West with which I'm unfamiliar?" She turned to study a watercolor hanging on the wall.

Immediately, Alecia wondered what her mother would say if she ever heard one of her daughters suggesting that a grudge should be held. Forgive, forgive, was all Alecia had heard from her childhood up. Yet, the more she thought of it, the more ludicrous it was that they should be going to the Domier Ranch as though they were all long lost friends. She felt anger that she had been duped into this whole affair. She winced at the pricks of conscience from the resentment rising within her. But in spite of the painful pricks, she could not, and would not ever like Mr. Lavren Domier.

"An unwritten code? I guess you could call it that," he replied. After a moment he asked, "You been working up any new riding acts?"

Her throat went dry. "No, Rayne, I haven't." The words were cold, empty. "I found the last act too distressful to consider."

The moment the words were out, she regretted them. She was ashamed to admit she had returned his kisses freely. She turned to see the hurt in his eyes, just as Nancy walked in.

"Time to go?" she asked as she entered. "Why, Rayne Lassiter! What a wonderful surprise. What a treat to be escorted to the celebration by such a handsome guy."

Rayne stood to greet Nancy and to receive her motherly

hug. Alecia busied herself getting their wraps.

She had never seen Rayne drive anything other than the ranch trucks and was unprepared for the Mercedes coupe parked in Nancy's drive. Nancy urged her in first while Rayne held the door, and thereby, still suffering from her own mortification, she found herself shoulder-to-shoulder with him.

He visited amiably with them as he sped down the section line road leading to the Domier Ranch. Alecia was quiet as she watched his broad hands maneuvering the wheel. If Nancy wondered what was wrong between them, she was sweet enough not to say so.

The words, DOMIER RANCH were formed in tall wrought iron letters suspended over the drive entrance between two massive stone pillars. The majestic house that Alecia surveyed that day with Rayne, was even more elegant from the front entrance. The sloping manicured lawns, were edged with well-tended flower beds and shrubbery. Not until Rayne led the two of them up the broad front steps did Alecia recognize where she had seen this portico before—in the photo in Joanna's bedroom. She experienced a strange sensation, wondering what memories this place held for Rayne.

A thin, dark-suited gentleman at the door gave them a colorless greeting, invited them in, and took their wraps. The entry hall was graced by a sweeping curved stairway and glittering crystal chandelier. Although Alecia did not remember seeing pumps on the Domier land, she now presumed his money came more from oil than from cattle.

Before the wispy man could show them to where the festivities were taking place, Lavren descended the carpeted steps on cat feet, head held high and a humorless smile pasted on his face. His ebony suit highlighted his iron gray hair, and if his manner were not so obnoxious, Alecia reasoned that he could be almost handsome.

"What an interesting group we have here," he said as he approached them. "I'll have to begin checking Corrine's invitation lists for these events a bit more closely. Never mind, Boyce," he waved the man back to his post at the door. "I'll show these fine people back to the party."

"Well, well, Lassiter," he rambled on, failing to greet any of them personally. "What could this party possibly offer to bring you out, fit to kill, during branding time?" As he spoke, he let his gaze fall upon Alecia, so that all concerned would know what he was implying.

Rayne and Nancy ignored Lavren's remark, but Alecia's face was ablaze with indignation. Whatever possessed Nancy to want to come here and endure this sarcasm?

Stepping through wide double doors to the spacious room filled with partygoers, Alecia tried to imagine Lavren and Corrine at home alone in this large house. Tall, stately windows were dressed in crimson velvet-corded drapes. Ornately carved, recessed ceilings glowed with muted indirect lighting. Smaller white colonnades repeated the theme of the portico, both in this room, and in the adjoining one from which were floating melodic strains of a dance number executed by a live orchestra.

In vain, Alecia searched the opulent furnishings for signs of Corrine's personal touch, but found none. In fact, had there been no warm sounds of romantic music, or laughter and easy conversation, the house would have resembled a cold museum.

Being her usual gracious self, Nancy socialized among the guests for a time, with Rayne and Alecia in tow. Later, she found a comfortable settee and, after seating herself, said with a smile, "I'd better be wise and rest if I want to make it through this evening. Rayne, would you be a dear and finish introducing Alecia around?"

Instantly, Rayne took Alecia's hand and was assuring Nancy he would take care of her "baby sister." Alecia was relieved that even after her harsh comment to him, Rayne was still in high spirits.

As the two of them moved through the twittering crowd, it struck Alecia how hurt Galen would be if he saw her coupled up, however inadvertently, with Rayne. She sensed by the turning of heads among the guests, that they were causing a stir. What was it Galen had said about having no competition other than a horse?

Rayne was cordial as he steered her by her elbow through clumps of people, politely introducing her and drawing her into the thin conversations, ranging anywhere from race horses to ranch irrigation to politics. Alecia mentally checked off the personalities she had met: a Dallas newspaper columnist, two attorneys, a state senator, and several high ranking officials from the national horse show association of which Corrine was an active member. It was a far cry from the barbecue at Rayne's house. Now she realized what Nancy meant by a level of social life here she hadn't known existed.

Strangely enough, the hostess of this whole affair was nowhere to be seen. "Wasn't this supposed to be Corrine's party?" Alecia asked Rayne as they plucked hors d'oeuvres from a tray. "Where is she?"

"Probably down at the stables talking horses with anyone who will listen," he commented dryly. "It's all the girl can think about."

If Rayne were dissatisfied with his role of keeping company with Nancy's younger sister, he made no signs of showing it. At one point he surprised her by ushering her onto the golden hardwood dance floor and leading her in a flawless waltz. Her fingertips spread over the tweedy texture of his suit, sensing the muscular shoulder beneath it. The refreshing smell of his aftershave drifted over her as the gentle refrains of the music wove the two of them together. She smiled her amusement as she relaxed in his arms.

"Share the secret?" he asked.

She hesitated, unsure if she should tell what she was thinking. "I never imagined," she ventured cautiously, "when I first met you that you would be an accomplished dancer."

He looked at her in mock seriousness. "Really? Then it's very lucky you're here tonight."

"And please tell me, sir, why is that?" She knew he was teasing and leading her on, but she didn't care.

He glanced about as if to detect eavesdroppers. "Promise you won't tell the boys from Big D?"

"Scout's honor."

"This whole thing is staged."

"You don't say!"

"I do say. Usually there's just some bluegrass tunes, a few fiddlers, maybe a banjo or two, some tobacco spittin' and a little hoedown. But, out of sheer self-defense, we decided to stage a little spoof to dispel all the Yankee myths about us hicks."

Involuntarily, her laughter spilled out, mingling with and then rising above the overture that was playing. She hadn't planned to draw attention. It just happened that way. "And the dancing? What about your fine dancing?"

"Oh, yes. Well, luckily one Saturday morning at the feed store, I had the winning number on my bag of Calf-Gro, and won two lessons at Bertie Mae's Dance Parlor."

By now Alecia feared the tears from her laughter would streak her mascara. "And?" She pressed her lips together to suppress her mirth.

"Can't you guess? I've already had one of the two lessons!"

"Rayne, please," she tried to protest.

"What can I say? I humbly give all the praise to Bertie Mae," he added with a deep bow as the music ceased. He led her laughing from the dance floor. By the time they had danced several numbers, Rayne had drawn her close, laying his cheek against her hair. From deep within her, blossomed the same dizzying excitement that surfaced the day he kissed her.

Later in the evening, Alecia saw Corrine unobtrusively enter a side door. The girl was dressed in an off-the-shoulder moss green gown that complimented her cascade of red hair perfectly. The martini glass could have been part of her ensemble as it never left her hand. In spite of her beauty, Corrine lacked the warmth of a hostess. Most of her guests, she chose to ignore and she moved among them speaking to a select few.

Alecia was greatly surprised when the youthful redhead approached her and Rayne with a hand extended and her face wreathed in a bright smile. "Rayne, you came after all!" she exclaimed. "Thank you. And Miss Winland. Welcome."

Remembering the day she had nearly been run off the road by this headstrong girl, Alecia was now puzzled by her overt friendliness. "Since I'm out of the classroom now," Alecia said to her, "let's dispense with the 'Miss Winland' bit. I hear it in excess of a trillion times a day. Just 'Alecia,' please."

"Alecia it is then. And you've been filling in at

Charlesy, haven't you? You're J.D.'s teacher now."

As Alecia answered in the affirmative, she could sense the child's name rising up like a needle to a balloon, obliterating the enchanted spell that had held her and Rayne together on the dance floor.

Rayne glanced across the room. "Looks like someone wants to talk business with me," he said brusquely. "If you'll excuse me. I wouldn't want to bore you, Alecia. I'll be back shortly."

Corrine downed her drink and caught a passing waiter to take another. "Want one?" she offered Alecia.

"I'd love a ginger ale."

Corrine gazed at her a moment. "Bring this lady a ginger ale," she instructed the waiter, then to Alecia, "You're something like your sis, aren't you? She won't touch the stuff either. Not a drop." She shook her mane of red hair. "Wish I could say the same thing."

Alecia changed the subject. "I want to congratulate you on your win. Nancy told me that's what this party's all about."

"Thanks." She sighed and seemed to relax some. "It's been a tough battle. Uphill all the way, but I'm finally getting there. I'm showing all of them. They didn't think I could do it. Didn't think I had it in me. But I'm showing them."

Alecia wondered if "them" was Lavren alone. It crossed her mind that she had not seen him since they first arrived. Odd host and hostess—throw a party then disappear. The waiter handed her the ginger ale and she sipped at its tanginess.

Corrine's hand was touching her arm. "Want to see her?" she asked.

Alecia failed to catch the meaning. "Her?"

"Twilight Song. My winning filly."

"Now?" To the stables in my heels? her mind asked incredulously.

"Sure, why not?"

Sensing the sincerity and intensity of Corrine's request, she relented. "Why not, indeed? Lead the way."

They set their drinks on a nearby table and slipped out the side door like children sneaking out of church. Corrine led her through a walnut-paneled study, down several halls, and down a flight of stairs before coming out onto a back patio at the lowest level.

Alecia stepped carefully over the rough gravel of the drive that led to the stables. In the moonlight, she could make out an enclosed pool and pool house far to their left across the sweeping lawn. Thankfully, the stable was not far. Alecia didn't think she could maneuver much farther in her heels.

Corrine stepped through a door and flung on a flood of lights that illuminated a stable nearly three times the size of Nancy's—all immaculately clean. And Corrine was probably spared the backbreaking job of mucking out stalls.

"Wait here," Corrine told her.

Alecia could hear nickering as Corrine spoke in quiet tones to the horse she brought out of a stall and led down the center area.

Twilight Song was a glossy, sorrel filly, brushed and groomed to a high sheen. Alecia's freshly born appreciation of fine horses sensed immediately that this was a winner. She reached out her hand to the lovely animal and Twilight Song never flinched at her touch. Like Kane Brake, she was gentle, yet regal.

"She's the most exquisite horse I've ever seen," Alecia

whispered in awe.

Corrine's expression glowed at the high praise. "Thanks. I trained her from a colt. She's sired by a national futurity winner and her dam is a race winner. She's an exceptional filly." She led the horse around in a few tight circles and Twilight Song seemed to sense she was on display, lifting her feet lightly and arching her neck proudly. "Some owners hire trainers," Corrine explained, "but I'm owner and trainer."

Alecia stroked the filly's glossy coat. "What a privilege to handle a horse of this caliber."

"Ted and Nancy's line was this good," Corrine confided. "They taught me a lot, and I appreciated all their help. I used to go over there after school when I was teenager." She paused. "I still miss Ted. He was sort of the father image I never had. I cried when Nancy had to sell the horses, but of course she had no choice. The cattle provided a more settled income for her."

Alecia chided herself for thinking Nancy and Corrine had nothing in common. She had no idea they had been close in years past. Could it be because of Corrine that Nancy fought back against Lavren no more than she did?

Corrine deftly led Twilight Song back to her stall, picking up her long skirt as she went. Her red hair shone in the lights of the stable and Alecia thought it a pity that Lavren could not see and appreciate his wife's beauty and talents.

"I'm glad you came this evening," Corrine said, returning to where Alecia waited at the door. "I've been looking for an opportunity to thank you. To be truthful, it was my ulterior motive in bringing you out here."

Alecia's mind went blank. "Thank me? For what?"

"For touching Joanna in such a special way. She's my

niece, you know."

"So I've learned."

"Did you also learn that Rayne will hardly let me near her? But she and I, we sort of find ways. She told me about the dress and about her play part. She's very excited."

Alecia faltered. "I'm sorry about the dress. That was a mistake, I'm afraid. I should have—"

"No, you were right about the dress." Corrine's green eyes glowed with pleasure. "Rayne's wrong in keeping such a tight hold on Joanna, but he won't listen. Just like I wouldn't listen when people warned me not to marry Lavren."

She stepped outside and held the door for Alecia. "See out there?" Corrine pointed to a rubble of foundation laid over with charred planks of wood strewn about. "That's where Darlene died."

"Darlene?" Alecia was shocked. "Joanna's mother?"

Corrine nodded, her lips going tight and pale. "My own sister. She was a wild one. I don't know why Rayne loved her so. She was wild and carefree. A lousy mother and rotten wife." She flipped her red curls back over shoulder as she spoke. "Seemed like a raw deal to me, for her to have such a wonderful family and treat them like dirt. And me. . . ." The words were left hanging in the still night air. Her young shoulders rose and fell in a deep sigh. "Rayne tried his best, but he couldn't tame her. They found her charred body in the bed there in the cabin along with Lavren's top foreman. Reedy, they called him. . .very handsome." She shook her head. "There was some kind of gas explosion and fire. Horrible, just horrible."

Alecia stared in unbelief at the rubble, awash in pale moonlight, and wondered why it hadn't been cleared away and built upon to remove the awful memories. So even

Nancy had known the ugly truth, but was unwilling to share it with her.

"It nearly destroyed Rayne when he found out." Corrine's voice was controlled, steady. "He was crushed. We saw him gradually change, retreating into his work and losing himself in the ranch. He's kept Joanna close to him, putting her in a cocoon for safekeeping, insuring he won't get hurt again. He's frightened she'll become like her mother if he releases her." She gave a wry smile. "But of course he refuses to admit that. I used to try to tell him, and now he hardly talks to me at all."

Alecia nodded mutely, thinking how she had ignorantly tread upon his open wound in her brashness. "Why are you telling me this?"

"Rayne hasn't been in our house since the fire." Corrine switched off the lights and closed the stable door behind them. "But he called me this week to find out if you were coming. It appears you may be the one he will listen to."

These truths were hitting Alecia's mind like live electric volts. If Rayne hadn't been in the Domier home for five years, that explained the turning of heads at the party. But why with her?

"I thought perhaps if Rayne heard truth coming from a new voice," Corrine went on, "he might see his mistakes. Joanna's going to be beautiful like Darlene. But she's nothing like her mother. There's none of that rebellion in her."

"No," Alecia agreed. "There's a sweet tenderness there."

"You see it, too?" There was a short laugh edged with relief. "Sometimes I get to thinking it's my imagination since she's my niece."

Alecia smiled softly, thinking of Joanna. "I see it, too."

Corrine moved toward the rubble of the ranch foreman's cabin, still talking. Alecia wondered how long these tormenting thoughts had been tamped down in Corrine's mind with no one to talk to.

"Not only did Darlene wreak havoc during her lifetime, she's continued to do so every day since her death."

"In what way?"

"Because of her miserable reputation, I've been accused of being just like her. Not an easy stigma to live down.

And my own husband is the worst of them all. We'd been married only a few months when he learned the truth about Darlene. From then until now, he's never given me a chance to be myself. I have to fight for everything I do here. He treats me like a child."

That was as Alecia had suspected from her brief observations.

"He uses whatever methods he can to hurt me. He attacks Nancy and harasses her because she's my friend. He uses other women to try to make me jealous. It's never ending."

"Why do you stay?" Alecia wanted to know.

Corrine thought a while. "Look at that house," she pointed to where the mansion stood basking in the moonlight. "It's not a bad place to live. And where else would I get to work with such prime horses?" She stopped again. Alecia waited. "Besides all that, I love the guy." She gave a shaky laugh. "Silly, isn't it? I've loved him ever since I was a little girl. And I believe, deep down, if he would stop all his agitating and fighting, he would learn he loves me, too. Maybe he's afraid to trust himself to love me for fear he would lose me like Rayne lost Darlene." She gave a little shrug. "Who knows what twisted things get inside of a person's head?"

The ringing of a phone in the stable froze her question in midair. Corrine lifted her skirt and hurried inside to answer the call. When she returned she said, "More reporters have arrived. They want to ask questions and take photos of the party. I've got to get back. Coming?"

"If you don't mind," Alecia said, "I think I'll stay out a few more minutes. The cigarette smoke was getting to me anyway."

"Sure thing." She turned to go, then over her shoulder added, "Thanks for listening."

Conflicting thoughts plagued Alecia as she strolled back toward the rubble to stare at the remains of the devastation. Some of what Corrine told her confirmed assumptions she had made previously. Other things were totally baffling. Some of Rayne's actions were more understandable now, but she puzzled why he stopped by to get her and Nancy. She didn't dare think it was only because of her. That was too amazing. Too confusing.

"Fitting burial monument, wouldn't you agree?" A low, raspy voice spoke behind her, startling and alarming her. She gasped aloud, whirling around to see Lavren Domier standing in the shadows of the stable.

eight

Fear and anger formed an acid taste in Alecia's mouth. It was exactly as Lavren had done at the Research Center—slithering quiet as a snake. Only this time there were even fewer people around.

"I've left this as a fitting monument to the wickedness of hard women." His formidable presence moved close beside her and she felt the flesh of her arms crawl. His voice was hard, bitter. The stench of liquor was heavy. "She was a hard woman." He stared glassy eyed at the wreckage. "So beautiful. So wicked. So hard." His voice wavered as one who had drunk too much. "I loved her first. Little Corrine didn't say that did she? She still doesn't know. Yeah, I loved her first. But Darlene enjoyed playing both ends against the middle, so she went to Rayne. But she didn't love him either. Made fools of both of us."

Alecia sensed his proud shoulders slumping under the weight of the ugly memories. First Corrine, and now Lavren opening up. What a bizarre evening!

"She dumped us both and took dumb, old Reedy." Lavren's hollow laugh echoed into the night air. "But that did her in. Died right here on my land. And she deserved to die," he added sharply.

Alecia's frantic mind sought for an easy way to escape while he was deep in his melancholy musings. Gently, quietly, she took one step back from him, then another.

"So I took second best," he mumbled on. "Took little

sister. Another wild one who thinks of nothing but horses. They're none of them like you, Alecia. You're so. . . ." He turned, and abruptly the slurred speech was accelerated as he grabbed for her arm. "Don't go!" he pleaded. "Please, don't leave me. I need you. You're not hard or rough. You're soft. . .tender. . .caring. . . ." His fingers sank cruelly into the flesh of her arm.

"Lavren, let me go! You're hurting me!" No one would hear her cries over the sounds of the music and the party. She had to get away. Her mind was wild with panic. She had no idea what he might do in this state.

"Please, Alecia," he begged, pulling her forcibly to him. She felt the heat of his breath on her neck, her face, repeating her name over and over as he held her in his strong grasp. Frantically, she jerked her head from side to side to get away from the fetid breath, the hard lips bruising hers.

"You blind, wretched ogre. Let me go. You don't deserve Corrine's love. You're consumed with hate and bitterness."

Unhearing, he began to pull her toward the stables. As he moved his handholds to lift her bodily into his arms, she kicked at his shin with all her might and broke from his grasp. She heard him yell as she pulled away and ran toward the house, kicking out of her shoes as she ran. *Dear God, help me,* her mind screamed silently.

Her sides heaved with sharp stabs of pain. Where was the entry where she had come out? She remembered the patio. If only she had gone back with Corrine. She heard no footsteps behind her, but was too filled with fear to slow down and look back. The house cast a looming shadow over the patio and she cautiously moved into its darkness, feeling for the doorway. When she slammed into a soft form, she screamed uncontrollably.

"Alecia! It's Rayne! What's happened to you? Who did this?"

"Lavren," was all she could say before collapsing into racking sobs released into his chest with his arms tenderly about her. Gently, he lifted her into his arms and took her around the house to his car. "I'll take you home," he told her, "then come back for Nancy. I'll take care of Domier later."

The promise made little difference to her. She was safe now and that was all that mattered. In the car he held her to him until her tremors ceased to convulse her body. Once again he transmitted to her his tender strength.

Everyone was embarrassingly apologetic. Rayne. Corrine. Nancy. Nancy, especially, was distraught about the entire mess.

"I had no idea," she told Alecia later, "that Lavren would ever harm anyone. I suppose I underestimated the poison that has festered inside him. From the beginning, I should have told you about Darlene's death, but I despise gossip, and have always tried to protect Corrine."

When Corrine learned of her husband's violence, she phoned to personally apologize. Rayne, of course, went back to the Domiers' that night to settle matters, but Lavren was nowhere to be found. By the time he reappeared, Rayne's anger had cooled, and Lavren conveniently remembered nothing of the incident.

Alecia wanted only to let it drop and hear no more of it. She was grateful that she had not been hurt. Grateful it was all over. And even grateful that her best shoes had been returned.

In her free time, she began to gather her possessions

together in preparation to leave. In time, all of this would be a blurred memory. There had been several happenings recently that she had been unable to tell Galen about over the phone. At times, long lapses of silence took over the conversation. Uncomfortable lapses. It bothered her.

On the night of the play, Mrs. Dominique baked her famous cinnamon rolls—high, light, and shiny with sticky white glaze. She served them with coffee to the parents who had brought their children early for costuming.

Alecia was busy in the girls' dressing room, flitting from one young actress to the other, touching up hair and makeup, and failed to see Rayne when he arrived to see the play.

She had been thankful for her heavy schedule leading up to the play and the last day of school. That way she could somehow function in the midst of a fog of uncertainty and vacillating feelings warring in her heart and mind.

Try as she might, she couldn't shake free of the thoughts of Rayne's alluring low voice near her ear, his sweet touch, his captivating manner. Guiltily, she found herself humming the melodies to which they had so effortlessly danced together.

"Miss Winland," a small voice demanded. "Aren't you going to help me?" Joanna was looking up at her with questioning eyes. She had changed from her blue jeans into her calico dress with the flowing skirt, flounced front, and puffed sleeves. She was ready for her hairpiece and her makeup. Flossie had purchased darling hairpieces consisting of long curls that the girls could tuck into their lace caps.

The dressing room was noisier now, and she and Flossie were having difficulty keeping the girls quiet. Lyle was in the other room, taking care of the boys. She could hear the commotion of the sixth-grade boys on the stage preparing the sets. The air was static with the kind of excitement that only children can create.

"What do you think Daddy will say when he sees me?" Joanna asked as Alecia applied the finishing touches of color to the girl's cheeks to prevent a washed-out appearance under the stage lights.

"He may not come right out and say so, Joanna," she said, using a whisper so the other kids couldn't hear her use the name. It was still their secret. "But he can't deny that you look perfectly lovely. Have you told him about your play part?"

"No," she answered with a mischievous grin. "I just told him there was a special program. He doesn't even know it's a play."

Alecia trembled as she adjusted the lace cap over the curls. The child looked incredibly like her mother. Perhaps, she thought, when Rayne sees her looking this lovely, really sees her, this night could be a turning point. How wonderful for her to go back to Minneapolis, knowing everything was all right in Joanna's life.

Once the curtains were opened and the play commenced, Alecia was kept busy backstage with costume changes and set adjustments. Flossie, who loyally sat behind the curtains and prompted the cast, said the entire play was flawless. Alecia knew only that the gymnasium was packed, with standing room only, and that she heard much laughter and applause.

It seemed only a few minutes before she was again assisting the girls out of costumes and back into their regular clothes. Parents were hugging her and commenting how wonderful the show had been and that they never realized such a production could be done with so small a space and so few supplies.

It was some time before it dawned on Alecia that Joanna's clothes were still lying across a folding chair in the dressing room. Nancy was at the door, her expression troubled. "He's taking her out, Alecia. He's leaving."

He couldn't. He wouldn't. Not after—not now! Wild thoughts rolled about in her head in a silent tumult. She grabbed up the clothes and ran out into the parking lot. The other parents were noisily enjoying Mrs. Dominique's rolls in the cafeteria.

There he was at the door of the pickup. Bewildered Joanna was already seated on the rider's side.

"Rayne!" she called out boldly.

He stopped and stared at her. His face was drawn and pale.

"Joanna's clothes," she said, using the given name in her haste and in her hurt.

He moved toward her as though in a trance. "I thought I could trust you," he said, his voice distant and detached as she pushed the clothes into his arms. "I thought I could trust you," he repeated the awful words. "But I should have known."

"Rayne, I didn't—"

"Don't bother to explain. Directly or indirectly, you were at the bottom of all this. This is what you've worked for all this time, isn't it? This was the final touch. The crowning glory. The final encore before you leave this forsaken little place where you've had to work out your psychological experiments on the local folks." The dark eyes were now glaring. "Have a fast trip back to the north country. Don't let anything slow you down."

The pickup door slammed on her pitiful protests to his accusations. Now it was his turn to spit gravel as he gunned the truck from the parking lot.

She stood there, paralyzed in a broken dejection that deadened all her senses. In a grief-filled haze, she forced her feet to move back to the jubilant crowd in the cafeteria.

She remembered what Corrine had said about how desperately Rayne loved Darlene. Alecia tried to imagine what it was like for him to see her almost resurrected in Joanna's face and appearance tonight.

"Don't punish yourself," Nancy begged her as they drove home from the play. "You couldn't help what happened."

Alecia was physically and mentally exhausted. "But he was right this time, Nancy. I did want to knock the prideful chip off his shoulder and I did want him to see things my way. I could have prevented Joanna from getting the part." Nancy had kindly offered to drive home and, as she did, Alecia stared at shadowy objects passing in the darkness. "How I wish I had. Not getting the part would have been far less painful for the child than to see her father in a rage. I'm to blame. I wanted him to see what was right, and succeeded only in being self-righteous."

After a night of fitful sleep, she dreaded facing her last day at Charlesy, which was to be a half-day session. As she had expected, Joanna was not present. Still, she was more grieved than she thought possible at being unable to say goodbye to her. They had talked about exchanging letters, but she had never given Joanna her address. No doubt Rayne would forbid such goings on.

Joanna. Precious Joanna Darlene. Why had she loved her so deeply?

Alecia had one last party with her students, laughing and telling jokes together. Several of the girls cried and begged Alecia to please come back to Oklahoma next fall to be their teacher.

She explained to them once again that she had a home and a job far, far away from Charlesy School, Denlin County, Oklahoma. And that she was homesick and anxious to get back. They couldn't understand. All they knew was that they wanted her to stay.

Mrs. Dominique prepared cold cuts for the staff who would be spending the afternoon cleaning and sorting. The elderly cook was also cleaning out her kitchen in preparation for its summer repose.

Alecia was working at a hurried pace when Lyle came into their classroom after having returned from the bus route. Again, he thanked her and assured her that she had opened many doors for future activities in the school by her endeavors. "All the parents were ecstatic about the play. It was an overwhelming success."

She pulled another pushpin from the bulletin board, releasing a bright posterboard flower. "All but one," she remarked dryly.

"I'm very sorry about Lassiter." His understanding was soothing.

"So am I," she countered.

"You even had me thinking we could make him see things differently. That's why I voted for J.D. to get the part. I guess it was too much to hope for after all these years. That man is dead set in his ways."

Dead set in his ways? That was exactly what she thought at first. In the beginning, when she was unaware of the pain and suffering. . .the deep inner wounds. Alecia pointed to a large box on the floor. "Want to help carry these to my car?" She put the last of the bulletin board decorations in the storage closet.

"Sure."

Together, they loaded the car with her belongings. In the May sunshine the aged stones of the schoolhouse seemed to glow. She looked at it as though she had never seen it before, pondering its long history and rich heritage. How many other such schools across this nation helped to form the country into what it is today? Funny she should think of that now, after she had disdained it so.

Lyle extended his hand. She took it. "Goodbye, Miss Winland," he said warmly. "If you're ever down on a visit, you know you're always welcome here."

She was unprepared for the misting in his eyes. Had she actually made that much of a contribution? It was all such a burden. She came so near to quitting...to throwing in the towel. "I don't feel I did all that much. As I look back, I only wish my heart had been more willing. I was struggling, you know."

He smiled. "I know."

"I think, perhaps," she slipped her sunglasses on her nose, "that I should be thanking you."

He stepped back as she put the small car in reverse and turned to drive out of the Charlesy school yard one last time.

Galen. She would call Galen as soon as she got to the house. She needed to hear his voice. That would stabilize her growing perplexities. When she got to Minneapolis, there would still be a week left of their school's session. That meant she would have opportunities to get caught up on details before the teachers scattered for the summer. Perfect. She would be busy, and Charlesy School, sitting like a golden island in the sea of emerald pastures, would be a mere memory.

The next morning, Nancy helped her pack. "Want to

take your blue jeans?" she asked with a wide grin. "Or are you going to leave them here for your next visit?"

Alecia was struggling with a box of old books that Mrs. Turner had given her after learning of Alecia's love for old readers. She seemed to be leaving with much more than she came with—in more ways than one. "Leave them," she said. "I can't jog or play tennis in them."

Alecia was scooting the box out the door of her room, when the phone rang. It was probably Galen asking when she would be leaving. She had been unable to get hold of him earlier and she was excited when she picked up the receiver. "Hello, there," she said lightly.

"Alecia?" It was Rayne. His voice was odd...strained. A piercing fear stabbed her stomach.

"Rayne? What's the matter?"

"It's Joanna." His voice caught. Never had she heard him say his daughter's given name.

nine

Alecia's knees went limp. She sat down in the chintz chair, nervously fingering the phone cord. "Rayne, what about Joanna? Where are you?"

"Denlin County Hospital in Kalado. Joanna's here. She was in the corral on her horse helping me cut out calves." He was able to say a few words, then faltered again. "The horse twisted somehow. . . ." His voice was trembling. "I don't know how it happened. She's an expert. The horse threw her and a horned steer gored her. . .threw her."

Alecia's heart pounded in her throat, strangling her. "What do the doctors say? What have they told you?" Little Joanna, her heart cried. Precious Joanna.

"She's in a semicoma now. "They've said. . . . Alecia?"

"Yes."

"Could you come? She. . . when she rouses, she asks for you."

Asks for me, Alecia thought. How wretched that must be for him on top of everything else.

"I'll be there soon as I can."

Alecia told Nancy bits and pieces of Rayne's report as she slipped into a clean dress, fluffed her hair, and threw a few things into her purse. "That's all I know," she said. "I'll call you later."

She paused at the front door thinking what else she might need. Then ran back to her room and grabbed her small Bible from out of her suitcase and tucked it into her purse.

124

When she stepped off the hospital elevator on the second floor, the acrid antiseptic odors sent her stomach churning. A nurse at the desk directed her to the hall where the room was located. Her heels beat a staccato rhythm as she scanned the doors for number 226. When she saw it, unconsciously, she began to tiptoe. She paused, then pushed at the heavy door that swung open noiselessly, revealing a bent-over Rayne sitting in a chair with his face buried in his hands. The bed was empty.

She studied him a few moments, then he glanced up and stood to his feet. He was still dressed in his work clothes, soiled blue jeans and faded shirt with the sleeves rolled up, exposing the sinewy tanned forearms with a tangle of masculine hair.

"Thanks for coming," he said. "I was afraid you'd left the country."

"I was just ready to leave."

"Will you stay?" he asked unapologetically. "For a while?"

She nodded, unable to speak, feeling totally incapable of helping him at this point. Silently, she prayed.

"They have her in emergency surgery. They told me I could wait in here." Reseating himself, he motioned for her to take the other chair. His voice was steadier now. "It was one of my longhorns. I have only a few. Something spooked them. They were acting nasty. All riled up." He leaned back in the chair and hooked a dirty boot over his other knee. "That crazy kid took off in there to settle them down, but. . . ."

Alecia's mind repulsed at hearing the details. She couldn't bear to think of that vulnerable little body at the mercy of horns and hooves. It wasn't fair. Couldn't he see how unfair it was? She wanted to scream at him of the unfairness of it all. Her nails bit sharply into her palms.

"I didn't see her fall. Don't know how she lost her balance. Sammy and I, we heard her scream and saw the steer get her and fling. . . ."

Alecia's breath caught as her stomach wrenched.

"Mr. Lassiter?" A uniformed nurse appeared at the door.

Rayne rose quickly. "Yes?"

"Your daughter is in the recovery room now. The doctor said to tell you the laceration was not serious. No vital organs were seriously injured."

Rayne nodded, his expression grim.

"However, she's not completely out of danger. The doctor will explain everything when he comes. She's had quite a blow to the head and has a badly broken ankle."

The nurse turned to Alecia. "Are you Mrs. Lassiter?"

"No," Rayne answered for her. "She's a friend. Joanna's teacher, actually."

Alecia was amazed to hear him use his daughter's name for the second time.

The straight-faced nurse raised her eyebrows. "I see. Well, the two of you might just as well get something to eat. She'll be in recovery for a time. We can call you as soon as she's returned to the room." She left the room, closing the door behind her.

Rayne looked at Alecia. "Want to get something?"

"It's up to you. Think you can?" Actually it was her own stomach she was thinking of.

"Beats waiting in this place." He took her arm and, through the myriad of halls, they found their way to the cafeteria on the first floor. The food aromas reminded Alecia that in her rush to get packed, she had not eaten for several hours.

Over the cafeteria vegetable soup, which they agreed wasn't too bad, they talked of mundane things that painlessly skirted issues that were too touchy to approach.

As they were finishing, a call came over the intercom for Rayne. He took it at the counter where he was informed that Joanna was being taken to her room.

Mentally, Alecia attempted to bolster herself as they returned to the room. She must not collapse or give way to emotions. Rayne would need her to be calm.

Joanna's surgeon met them in the hall as they approached the room. He was a young man with wire-rimmed glasses and kind eyes. "Mr. Lassiter, I'd like to talk with you for a moment."

Alecia felt Rayne grope for her hand and clasp it tight. "Yes, sir," he answered.

"Your daughter came through the surgery nicely. The wound was not so bad as we originally thought. Miraculously, the horn did not puncture any vital organs. However, the next few days will be touch and go. We'll be keeping close watch on her."

The grip on Alecia's hand tightened. "Are you saying we could still lose her?" The words were soft.

The doctor place a gentle hand on Rayne's massive shoulder. "That's exactly what I'm saying, Mr. Lassiter. It was a powerful impact to her head."

"Has she regained consciousness?"

"Not yet, but we feel she will soon."

"Can I see her now?"

The young doctor nodded and stepped aside.

Rayne released Alecia's hand at the door. She saw him stagger as if from a blow when he saw his daughter lying there. Her tiny ashen face was crowned in a swath of pure white bandage, thin arms penetrated by needles and tubes, an exposed leg encased in a cast from the shin down. But he righted himself and moved toward the bed.

"Joanna. Hey, sugar." The voice was full of tender love. "You're gonna be all right. Daddy's here. I'll be right here whenever you need me."

Alecia watched, scarcely able to contain the surging emotions within her at the sight of his broad, calloused hands touching the child's pale cheek. There was no response.

Nurses came in at intervals to take her vital signs. Rayne walked about the room, sat down for moments, then moved back to Joanna's side to touch her, speak to her, check her breathing.

Throughout the afternoon and evening, there were many calls. "No," Rayne told them patiently. "No change. There's nothing you can do now. No, don't bother to come. We just have to wait."

When Josie called, Alecia could hear the woman's strong voice from where she was sitting across the room. The hearty old queen of El Crosse was distraught that her little charge was in danger. It occurred to Alecia that Josie might have taken care of Rayne when he was Joanna's age. No telling how long she had been with the family.

"Get those men fed tonight, Josie," Rayne told her. "Keep them in line and tell Sammy to get them all on the job in the morning. Then you and Sammy come up here tomorrow. Nothing you can do now."

As Rayne was talking, there came a soft knock on the open door. Alecia looked up to see Nancy's pastor, Joe Bob, standing there. She rose to greet him, thankful for a familiar face.

Presently, Rayne hung up the phone and came to the door with an extended hand. "Joe Bob Tygert. Haven't seen you in a long while."

"How've you been, Rayne?" The two exchanged a firm handshake.

"You know Alecia Winland," Rayne said. "She's Joanna's teacher at Charlesy School."

"Sure do," Joe Bob said. "She's been one of my parishioners ever since she arrived in Denlin County."

A brief expression of surprise registered on Rayne's face. "Oh yeah, sure," he said quickly.

"How is Joanna?" the pastor wanted to know.

Rayne parroted what the doctor told him earlier. His voice was hollow as he spoke.

Joe Bob ran his fingers through his curly hair. "Mind if we pray about it?"

Immediately, Alecia sensed Rayne's discomfort. Before he could speak, she said, "It couldn't hurt."

Rayne then nodded, his lips pressed tightly together.

Joe Bob's affable manner took no offense. He stepped to Joanna's bedside and placed his hands on her tiny arm and softly spoke to the Father God in her behalf. He included Joanna's father as well, praying for the "peace that passes understanding," to cover him during this time.

As Joe Bob prepared to leave, Rayne asked, "How'd you happen to stop by?"

The good-natured fellow smiled. "I could say that I was on my rounds and happened to see the name Lassiter on the New Patient list. The name does kind of jump out at people around here." He gave a friendly grin. "But truthfully, Nancy called the house after Alecia left, to ask church members to be praying. I thought I would come by to see if you needed anything. Haven't seen much of you for the past few years."

Rayne hooked a thumb in the pocket of his blue jeans.

"Our paths split. . .once you chose preaching over ranching."

"My daddy says the very same thing," Joe Bob countered.

They were standing in the hall now and Alecia was surprised to hear Rayne release a light chuckle. Joe Bob had his ways.

"You know," the pastor drawled, "I once thought you and I were gonna get real close. Remember when you were madly in love with my kid sister in sixth grade?"

Alecia smiled, trying to imagine Rayne as a sixth-grader.

"She jilted me," Rayne quipped.

"She told me it was because of them ugly bowed legs of yours," Joe Bob teased.

Rayne shook his head. "Could have been. Or else the fact that I ate the chocolate chip cookies out of her lunch pail every noon hour."

"Mama did make scrumptious chocolate chip cookies. Say, why don't you come on over to church some Sunday? We'd love to have you."

"Church?" Rayne studied the geometric floor tiles, then looked up at Joe Bob. "No. No church. Not for a while yet. Maybe someday. Maybe."

Joe Bob reached out for Rayne's hand. "Alecia has our number if you need us. We're as near as the phone."

Rayne, suddenly mute again, only nodded. He and Alecia returned to the room as the pastor's footsteps echoed down the hall.

Later that evening, the calls ceased, and it grew hushed and still in the room. Somewhere in the ward, a baby cried and a child called for his mother. But Joanna lay in deathlike silence.

Minutes crept by endlessly. The nurses' bantering out in the hall extended to them a comforting effect, assuring them that there was yet a measure of normality in the universe.

The two of them took turns milking coffee from the impersonal canteen machine down the hall in the waiting room. It tasted terrible, but it kept them awake.

Once, the voices and noises faded far into a vague, muffled distance. Alecia started, realizing she had dozed off. She awakened to see Rayne staring out the window at a sky ablaze with spangles of stars. His expression was strained, almost colorless. When would he break and release the awful torment that was fermenting within him? Was she to press in and assist, or simply wait?

She wanted to tell him how wrong she had been. She wanted to confess to him her horrid self-righteousness. But was this the right time? She remembered what Nancy said about letting him come to grips with things in his own way...his own time. This time she wanted it to be God's move, not hers.

At length, he turned and looked at her. "My turn to get coffee," he said. Before leaving, he stepped into the restroom and splashed cold water on his face.

He had been gone only a moment when she heard it. A faint, feeble sound. "Miss Winland." The brown eyes were fluttering open, struggling to focus. "Miss Winland?" she murmured weakly.

"Yes, Joanna. I'm here. Your Daddy's here, too. Down the hall."

"I was good. Good...Betsy Ross." The words came slowly, spaced apart, weak. Oh, so weak. Like a silver thread that would snap at the mere touch.

"You were marvelous, Joanna." Hot tears momentarily

blinded Alecia. "I was so very proud of you."

The lashes fluttered again. Her eyes met Alecia's for a fraction of a moment and a slight smile glimmered. "Good Betsy," she repeated. "The. . .best."

That was all. Silence pulled its blanket back over her. The breathing fell back to its slow, steady rhythm.

Was it for this moment she had been prevented from quitting Charlesy and returning home early? Thanks be to God for His dear guiding hand.

When Rayne returned and looked at Alecia's face, he knew immediately. "What is it?" he asked anxiously, placing the steaming cups on the dresser.

"She spoke."

He stepped over to the bed, looking, hoping. Not touching, just looking. "She ask for you?"

Alecia couldn't speak over the knot in her throat. "Uh huh," she whispered.

"What did she say?"

Alecia knew she could easily lie and he would never know the difference. Why heap fresh new pain upon the old?

"I can take it," he said grimly, not taking his eyes off the child. "What did she say?"

Alecia drew a breath. "She said she was a good Betsy Ross." Her voice cracked. "The best."

Rayne's eyes closed and for a moment, Alecia thought he was going to fall over in a faint.

The if onlys must be screaming their relentless indictments at him now. "Oh Lord," she prayed silently, "let the dam within him give way and spill out the ugly contents."

Dawn streamed in the tall windows, contradictively joyous and golden. It awakened Alecia who had, once again, dozed. She excused herself to the ladies' room down the hall to freshen up her makeup and hair. When she returned to the room, Josie and Sammy were there. Josie was leaning over Joanna, crying softly. "Sweet baby. My sweet, sweet baby," she repeated over and over, stroking Joanna's face.

Alecia sensed that her release of emotions was making it extremely difficult for Rayne. She grabbed up the satchel of clean clothes Josie had brought and handed it to him. "Here," she said. "Josie brought this for you. Why don't you go change and freshen up?"

The soft brown eyes thanked her. He took the satchel and left without speaking.

Sammy stood uncomfortably, twisting his hat in his hands. He wiped a tear off his sandpapery cheek with the sleeve of his worn cotton shirt. Kindly, Alecia urged him to sit down and he perched his lanky body on the edge of the orange vinyl hospital chair as though it were a rattlesnake's den.

Rayne returned looking somewhat collected. He managed to give Alecia a weak smile.

Josie and Sammy left, but others began dropping by. Lyle and Flossie. Rancher neighbors, some she knew, others she had never met. At first, Alecia excused herself when people came, but Rayne asked her to please stay. She wondered if they thought it strange that she should be there in the room with them.

She was delighted to meet Rayne's father who greeted her with open warmth. "I've heard J.D. make mention of you on several occasions," he commented after Rayne introduced them. "All good," he added.

Roland Lassiter, impervious to age, stood straight and tall as Rayne. His dark eyes, not wide and expressive like

Rayne's, were nonetheless kind and shed open, unchecked tears at his granddaughter's bedside. The silver-haired Lassiter appeared to be so independent. Alecia marveled that he had so completely given over the reins of El Crosse to his son.

Watching him, Alecia for the first time became curious about Rayne's mother. . .her personality and how she had fit into the meshwork of the story of the ranch. It certainly wasn't the proper time to ask. She was sorry she had not asked sooner.

Nancy came by and brought the jonquil yellow dress for Alecia to change into. "Seems I remembered you said J.D. liked this one."

"Joanna," Alecia corrected her.

"Joanna?" There were raised eyebrows, but an excited smile on Nancy's face.

Alecia felt a surge of renewed vigor after changing, but by late afternoon the toll of the previous night began to tell on her. Weariness bound up in her bones, her body screamed for a bed.

She and Rayne were sparked to life by Corrine's arrival, dressed as usual in one of her striking western suits and matching hat. Her hair was fastened severely at the nape of her neck. Though concerned for her niece, she seemed to be in good spirits. She talked extensively with Rayne, wanting to know every detail. It seemed to Alecia that she asked more pertinent questions about Joanna's condition than any visitor so far.

As she was preparing to leave, Corrine asked Alecia to walk with her to the gift shop to pick out something for Joanna. Alecia looked at Rayne and he nodded.

True to Corrine's style, she purchased the fluffiest, most feminine looking stuffed kitten in the gift shop and wrote an endearing note on a card. "When she wakes up, tell her this is from her Aunt Corrine," she instructed.

"My pleasure," Alecia assured her. How comforting to hear her say "When she wakes up."

As they approached the elevator, Corrine drew her into an empty waiting room. "Before I go," she said, lowering her voice mysteriously, "there's something I must tell you. It may only be a case of overblown imagination but there seems to be a change in Lavren."

"In what way?" Alecia attempted to be polite, but hated to even discuss the situation.

"First, I must explain that Lavren did say he forgot all that happened that night out at the stables. As stoned as he was, I don't doubt it. But he did mention one thing you said."

Alecia frowned, remembering the horrible moment when she was so frightened. "What was that?" she asked with some apprehension. Perhaps he had made up something to alleviate his guilt.

Corrine's pretty lips held a vague smile. "He said he remembered your yelling at him that he didn't deserve my love and my affection. Strange as this may sound, I don't think it ever occurred to him that I might love him." She firmed the hat on her head. "And now. . .well, now he seems a little different somehow. We'll see."

Alecia took a breath. "Corrine, I must confess to you that I've not prayed for Lavren as I should have. I let my anger against him take precedence over my need to pray for him. But I want you to know, from this moment on, I'll be praying for the two of you. You deserve to be happy. God meant for life to be enjoyed, not simply endured."

Corrine shrugged. "If you say so. All I've ever known was fight and struggle for everything. But thanks for the good word anyway. Oh, and just for the record," she grasped Alecia's arm, "Joanna will pull through this. I know what kind of stuff she's made of. She's a fighter."

Remembering Joanna's first words when she awakened in the night, Alecia had to agree. "She certainly is."

The sky outside the hospital window was pulling a curtain of lavender twilight when the phone rang in Joanna's room. Since Alecia was nearest, she took it.

"Alecia? Is that you? Nancy said you might be there." Galen's tone was harsh. "What is going on down there?"

"Galen. Oh, Galen. I'm so sorry. I completely forgot to call you." How could she have forgotten that she was supposed to be on her way back to Minneapolis this minute?

"Sorry? Sorry?" He was incredulous. "Alecia, I've been more than patient and understanding in this whole matter, but this beats all. What are you doing?"

Alecia could feel Rayne's curious stare on her back. "There's this little girl. . .one of my students. She was badly hurt. I'll be here a few days yet."

"A few days?" His voice rose in volume and pitch. She hoped Rayne couldn't hear him as plainly as she had heard Josie. "What is this child to you? Is she more important than the job that's been held for you these past months?" he demanded with indignation. "You were to be here for an important staff meeting on Friday. I had it all set up. Doesn't this child have any family? Where are they?"

Behind her, she heard Rayne step out of the room. What a gentleman. "Here. They're here."

"Then why, pray tell, are you needed? You can keep in touch with them by phone—like you've been doing with me," he added bitterly.

Alecia strained to collect her thoughts. To make herself

clear. To be understood. "I promised to stay."

"It isn't just the job, Alecia." His voice softened somewhat. "You should know that. I miss you so much I can hardly stand it. If the pressures were off here, I would have caught a flight out of here by now."

"I know. This little girl. . .she's special. I can't explain it. She's just very special. I'll leave soon. I'll contact you when I know for sure. I promise." But in truth, at this point, she had no idea when she would be leaving.

She heard him release a sigh. "I can't run your life. However, neither can I guarantee anything in the office from now on. I'll have to tell Harwood you won't be here for the Friday meeting and that you don't know when you'll be coming. It won't sound very good."

"It's the best I can do, Galen. And thank you." With trembling hand, she replaced the receiver in its cradle. "And the rest is up to you, Lord," she whispered.

Rayne asked nothing about the phone conversation and she offered nothing. Things were difficult enough for him without his knowing that her job was on the line because of the extended stay.

The sky outside the window was dark again, and clouds covered the stars. The lights of the town of Kalado twinkled in scattered profusion like so many lost fireflies. Nothing like the intensity of the Minneapolis skyline at night.

Rayne was restless. Such a small space for a cowboy to be cramped into, she thought. She had been reading the Psalms from her small Bible.

Abruptly, he turned to her. "You trust God, don't you?"

His words startled her. She closed the small leather-bound book and let it lay in her lap. "Yes, Rayne, I do."

"I mean trust. . .not just believe. Most everybody I know

believes there is a God. But you trust Him, don't you?"

She nodded. How could she explain to him that her Creator was her best Friend?

He paced to Joanna's bedside and back to the window. "Joanna's no better. And I think I need to pray. But I don't. . .I'm not sure He'll hear. I need your help."

"Of course. Whatever it is you need, I'll try to help."

He stepped over and drew the other chair close to her. "I know you've been praying all along. I can tell. I'm her father. I should be praying, too. But I can't." He shook his head. "I just can't."

She reached out to give his arm a reassuring touch.

"I'd like to go to the chapel," he said.

"Upstairs?" She couldn't imagine him wanting to leave the room. He had hardly left, other than a few minutes at a time, since Joanna came out of surgery.

"Will you come with me? It's important."

She slipped the Bible into the pocket of the yellow dress and stood. Possibly, the dam was cracking.

They informed the nurses at the desk where they were going. "We'll keep a close eye on her," one of them said with a kind smile.

Some benevolent person had left a full bouquet of pink carnations and lavender iris, laced with baby's breath, on the chapel's entry table. The fragrance wafted gently over them as they entered the small room. Brass wall lamps on each side, lent a soft glow. The small pews, altar, and pulpit were in rich hues of mahogany. Cushiony carpet beneath their feet was in stark contrast to the cold hospital room floor.

"It's almost spooky in here," Rayne said, closing the door behind them.

Alecia sat down on the front pew, thankful for the soft

comfort. Rayne remained standing, looking ill at ease and staring at the gold cross on the altar. Finally, he spoke, his tremulous voice betraying the strain. "What if. . .what if Joanna dies, never having worn the pretty dresses she needed to have?"

"Rayne, don't."

"And the baby dolls, the stuffed animals, hair ribbons, lockets. . . ." His voice broke off in a half-sob. "You were right and I couldn't bear to hear the truth. Corrine was right and I ordered her never to see Joanna again."

"Those things you named are important, but they're not everything."

"Don't pacify me now, Alecia. I've got to face the truth. Even if it's almost too late. In fear, I held on tight to her because she was all I had left in life. But even as I clung desperately to her, I could feel her slipping away."

Alecia slipped her hand into her pocket and clutched the Bible. "Even if you should lose Joanna this very night, still she's known all her life that her daddy loves her. Never, never has she had reason to doubt your love."

He shook his head. "I never even told her how wonderful her play part was. She was the best one there. When I saw her made up like that. . .looking so much like her mother. . . ." He was pacing now, his voice sharp with frustration. "Not little girllike anymore, but womanlike, I was filled with a new fear. A fear that she really would become like Darlene. That's why I turned her interests to the work at the ranch. In my own clumsy way, I tried to keep her the way I wanted her.

"My wife, Darlene, was devastatingly beautiful. I loved her with such a passion." He slapped his fist into his palm. "Then I hated her with an even greater passion. She destroyed all that she touched."

"She gave you Joanna," Alecia said simply.

Rayne turned and folded his tall frame, kneeling at her feet. "I don't want to hate her. It's eating me alive. It's destroying me. Because of hate, I couldn't bear to call Joanna by her right name, or to let her become the little lady she deserves to be."

"Forgive her," Alecia urged him. "Forgive Darlene."

He shook his head. The muted light from the brass lamp reflected a tear streak on his cheek. "It's too late. Too much damage has been done. You can't forgive a dead person. I'm locked in."

She touched the tear to dry it away. He caught her hand and pressed it to his face. "Help me, Alecia."

"You can pray and ask the Lord to forgive your hatred of her. For Him to take it away."

"He can do that?" The question held a note of wonder.

"And whatsoever ye shall ask in my name, that will I do," she quoted John 14:13. She brought out the Bible to show him the passage.

"But it's so hard to ask."

"When you want something so desperately, it's never too hard."

Rayne's gentle eyes searched hers for a moment. Then, he lay his head on her shoulder and surrendered over to the great ripping sobs that tore into the layers of pent-up bitterness and hate. His prayers, smothered in sobs, were heard by the One Who could touch the deep inner wounds that no man's hand could heal.

Gently, she stroked the dark, fine-textured hair and at long last, gave vent also to her own reservoir of awaiting tears.

Later, they would pray for Joanna Darlene. Together.

ten

There was yet another day of endless vigil before Joanna's brown eyes fluttered open. From the moment she awoke, she never stopped talking. And her father was overjoyed, joking that she would probably never be that still ever again. But Alecia knew he was ecstatic to have her back.

The doctors' reports were optimistic that full recovery was on the way. Joanna was taken off the IVs and was allowed to walk a short way—on her crutches—that very day.

Alecia wearily excused herself late that night to return to Nancy's and attempt to get one good night's sleep before leaving for Minneapolis the next morning. When she left the room, Rayne and Joanna were deep in conversation, pinpointing why she was thrown and what could have been done to prevent it. Alecia smiled inwardly, as her heart sang praises to God.

Following Galen's call, Alecia had located an isolated pay phone and called Mr. Harwood personally. She was pleased and thankful that he was willing to postpone the meeting. She took the opportunity to tell him the work she had done while she was away.

"That's what I like about you, Miss Winland," he commented in his gravelly voice, "you never miss a chance to further your skills."

Although she realized she could not take all the glory, she decided to leave it at that. She could fill him in on the details later.

It was easy for Alecia to see why Galen's patience with her faltered. Still, it left her with a hollow feeling that he had not been more understanding of her position. At the same moment, she chided herself—had their roles been reversed, would she have been as cooperative? She wasn't sure.

She slept like a baby in her room at Nancy's that night. Every bone in her body thanked her for the comfort of a real bed once again. The next morning, Nancy outdid herself preparing a delectable cheese and sausage omelette.

Loading the car took only a few minutes, during which time Nancy went on and on about how wonderful it was that Alecia had come to help. How she appreciated the company, the work, and the moral support. "I'm at a loss," she said as she swung the little overnight case into its nesting place in the full trunk, "to fully express my thanks to you. I can only pray that your time here will prove to benefit you for the rest of your life."

Alecia remembered what Mother had said. That if she gave of her time and energies, it would open the door for God to work His perfect will. She was certain Rayne's breakthrough was part of that perfect will and she was grateful she played a small part in it.

"I believe that our prayers are going to be answered to the fullest," Alecia assured her as they hugged goodbye.

As she drove slowly out of the drive of the Whitlow Ranch, she and Nancy frantically waved to one another like two teenagers parting at summer camp. There were moments when Alecia wondered how Nancy would fare alone, but her sister had regained much of her strength the past few weeks and was now back in the saddle, out keeping watch over her acres of pasturelands.

The glen at the twists in the road was cool and shady and curtained in an early morning mist. Alecia pulled her loaded car to a stop, hopped out, and stepped through the spongy grass to Jake's front door. "I stopped to tell you goodbye, Jake," she said as he opened the door.

"Jest like I told you," he answered with a wide grin. "I train me a good hand, then she ups and leaves." He stepped down out of the mobile home and extended to her his weathered hand. Shaking his head, he added, "I thought maybe you was getting sweet on the good looking Lassiter boy, and then we'd get to keep you."

Alecia succumbed to an unaccustomed blush. "Rayne and I? How silly," she scoffed. "We're worlds apart."

"Yeah, well, I've heard that's what makes marriage interesting," he drawled. "Anyway, that's what old Roland Lassiter used to say about his little gal from Philadelphia."

"Philadelphia? Rayne's mother? You're kidding."

"Naw." Jake scratched at a place on his shoulder where his shirt was threadbare. "Mrs. Lassiter was a high-bred gal who fell for an old rawhide rancher. Purty rough on her at first, but she finally got used to us." Pausing for a gaping yawn, he said, "Now you be sure to come back and see us sometime. Y'hear?"

"I will. And meanwhile, look out after Nancy for me. Y'hear?"

He gave a dry laugh. "Sure will, Miss Winland. That old bottle don't have such a tight hold on me now. I'm doing better, and I'll look after her. Don't worry."

As she drove away from his little home among the trees, Alecia thought about how Nancy trusted Jake when no one else would. Now, he was her friend for life.

Word had it that Josie was planning a big coming home

party for Joanna, even though they were not certain when she would be released from the hospital.

A part of Alecia wished she could be there for the gala celebration. If only she could have known Josie better...and Sammy, too, for that matter. And Roland. All of them suddenly seemed dear to her. They had each one been so patient with her. She couldn't wait to tell Delia about each and every one of them.

When she arrived at the hospital to give her last goodbye, Rayne met her outside Room 226. His eyes were dancing. "Can't go in yet," he cautioned. "Just a little surprise." Then realizing how silly he sounded, he added almost apologetically, "You know how it is with kids."

"I ought to," she countered with a grin.

"Is she out there?" came a call from inside the room.

"Yeah, she's here," Rayne called back, part and parcel to the game in progress.

"Make her wait a minute. I'm not ready."

"I'm holding her back with all my might, but she's struggling," Rayne answered, attracting the attention of passers-by."

"What is this? A conspiracy?" she accused, loving every minute of it. Rayne's countenance was aglow with joy.

"Okay," Joanna called, "let her in. I'm ready."

"This took a lot of hurrying and conniving," Rayne said aside to her as they went in. "I hope you realize what a privileged character you are."

Rayne opened the door upon Joanna decked out in the yellow dress from Archer's. Her massive head bandage had been replaced by a smaller one and the nurse had taped a yellow ribbon to it. Other than appearing a trifle pale, Joanna was lovely!

Alecia didn't have to pretend her pleasure and surprise at the unique sight of a little girl sitting in a hospital bed, dressed in a frilly frock. One foot sported a yellow sock, the other was still partially covered in a cast. "Joanna Darlene. How lovely you look."

"Daddy bought it for me. Can you believe it? Isn't he simply wonderful?" she said, giving a big wink.

Alecia joined in the joke. "Wonderful? Wonderful just isn't the word." She walked over and rubbed the silken cloth between her fingers. "Hasn't the man simply marvelous taste in ladies' fashion and fabric?"

Joanna giggled. "I say, he really does. It's a rare thing these days, wouldn't you agree?"

"Quite rare, quite rare," Alecia agreed, nodding vigorously.

"Hey, you two. Knock it off," Rayne protested. "You sure make it tough on a guy who's trying to apologize and say he's been wrong."

"I think he's crying uncle, Joanna. We'd better give him mercy," Alecia cautioned.

"Oh," Joanna cooed. "Come here, Daddy. I'm sorry. We were just kidding." She motioned for him to sit on the side of her bed, then put her arms around his neck. "I love the dress more than ever. Now I feel like it's from both of you."

She motioned for Alecia to come sit on the other side of her. "Besides, the nurses said I could only wear it for a few minutes, then I'll have to put my pajamas back on. This was a special surprise for your going away."

"Thanks, Joanna. Seeing you like this is the best present you could ever give me. You have my address. I expect to receive a letter from you."

"Will you write me back?" Joanna wanted to know.

"I sure will."

"Will you write Daddy, too?"

Alecia looked at Rayne. Looking into those deep eyes was difficult. She wondered what was really going on in there. "I don't know about that. We haven't had time to discuss it."

"He'll probably want to, now that you're pretty good friends," Joanna pronounced matter-of-factly, embarrassing the both of them.

"I must go now," Alecia said, shaking off the discomfort. "It's a long drive to Minneapolis. Goodbye, Joanna. I'm so thankful you're going to be totally well soon."

"Miss Winland, I love you." Joanna couldn't hold back the easy tears of youth. "You're the most wonderful teacher I've ever had. Please promise to come back and see me someday."

Alecia received the bear hug from the thin arms. "I promise. I will." She swallowed past the tightness rising in her throat.

"I'll walk you down," Rayne told her. To Joanna, he said, "You be back in those pajamas when I get back. You hear? Josie wants the dress fresh and clean for your coming home party."

"Do I have to take it off now?"

"Now," he answered, settling the matter.

Rayne walked quietly beside Alecia all the way to her car. The day was balmy and cotton puff clouds hung low in the baby-blanket blue sky. Alecia turned her face to the breeze to smell of its spring freshness. Already there had been hot days, warning of the humid Oklahoma summer to come.

"Alecia," Rayne said as they reached the car, "thank you for being a good friend to Joanna. I can see now how badly she needed someone like you. And I'm sorry for all the harsh things I said to you. I'm hoping you'll forgive me for being so ungrateful." He put his hand to the car door as though to open it, but let his hand rest there.

"It's done. I've already forgiven you. I said some harsh things to you, too. And what I didn't say openly, I was thinking to myself. Actually, I wasn't very fair with you. So the forgiving goes both ways."

"Most of what you said, I needed to hear," admitted Rayne. "You've helped me so much. The awful weight that I carried around for so long is gone. Really gone." His eyes were soft with wonder. "For the first time in years, I actually feel peaceful. I never thought it could be possible. You helped me to see that God's mercy could include me. I'm grateful."

"I didn't go about things very graciously at first. I suffered from a bad case of self-righteousness. It's not the best vehicle for displaying God's mercy. I wanted so much to see Joanna set free, that I ignorantly rubbed salt in your wounds."

"But," he insisted, "if you hadn't come at me with all that sass and spitfire, I may not have heard."

"You mean you did hear?"

"I heard all right. And it hurt like blazes. That's why I got so mad." He gave a wry smile.

"We came through a lot in a few short weeks, didn't we?" Her thoughts flew to the rainy day in the stable...to the night they floated together on the dance floor...the special time in the chapel. In a flash she recalled every word, every fragrance, every tender emotion.

"An awful lot," he agreed. He gazed out over the parking lot. He had forgotten to pick up his hat and it seemed strange to see him bareheaded outdoors. The dark hair was riffled slightly by the breeze. She remembered how silky it felt as his head lay on her shoulder and his tears streamed into the fabric of her dress.

He returned his gaze to her face. "I wish you could stay a while longer."

A while? What did he mean by a while? A while was such a vague term. It could mean an afternoon, a summer, a lifetime.

"It would be nice," she replied. "But I have a job waiting. . .and a lot of work as well."

"And Galen?" he asked.

The question surprised her. He had not mentioned Galen even after that awful phone call in Joanna's room that night.

"Yes, Galen," she admitted, squinting against the morning sun streaming through the puffy clouds. She rummaged in her shoulder bag for her sunglasses. "Galen Rustin is my working partner."

"Is that all?"

Why should he want to know this now? Such a silly time to talk of Galen. "Well, no, not exactly. He's a confidant, a close friend, and a Christian brother."

"I see." He took a quick breath.

"And before I left, we were seeing one another regularly on a social level"

She wished if he had something to say, he would say it. His hedging was difficult to handle.

"Well, teacher lady, you might drop us a line now and then. Let us know how you are."

Us, he had said, not me. "I will, Rayne. Remember now, if a teacher brings Joanna home from school, and if her car dies in your drive—beware!"

Her levity broke the tension and his warm deep laugh

sounded forth. "Thanks for the warning ma'am, but you're too late." He placed his arm about her shoulder and for a moment she feared that he might kiss her again. She knew she couldn't bear that at this moment. Instead, he tilted her chin, and placed an endearing peck on her nose. For a split second her heart cried out to hear him say, "Stay with me, Alecia. Stay with me forever!"

But, of course, he didn't. Of course, he didn't. And the next moment, she didn't even want him to. That was insane thinking. She had helped him see truth. He was grateful for her help. That's all there was to it.

He opened her car door and she settled herself in, perching the sunglasses on her nose. "Goodbye, teacher lady," he said softly. "Don't forget us."

"I never could. Goodbye, Oklahoma rancher."

The two-day drive, broken by an overnight stay in a quiet motel, gave ample time for idle pondering. Alecia assumed that as she stacked up the miles between her and Denlin County, the memories would diminish. On the contrary, they were growing larger in her mind.

Time, she reasoned. Time and activities will erase them. And, once again, she turned her thought to the work that awaited her.

It was late when she parked in the underground parking garage beneath her high-rise apartment building. She grabbed her few pieces of luggage and locked the car. She and Delia could lug the rest of it up the next day.

She rang the bell first. She didn't want to frighten Delia who had lived alone for four months now.

"Who is it?" Delia sang out.

"Me, silly. Your long lost roomie." Quickly, she was let in and there was as much hugging in coming home as there had been in leaving Oklahoma.

The two of them sat up and chatted until the wee hours of the morning. Delia had much to tell of new friends, a new promotion, and change of job position. Then, she wanted to know all about Denlin County. Alecia complied with her request, omitting a few of the more harrowing and touchy details.

When Alecia finally crashed into bed, she was determined to call Galen first thing the next morning. He would probably take the day off to spend with her.

"Good morning," she said brightly to him when he answered her ring just after the sun has risen. "I'm home. Arrived late last night."

"I thought you might call me first thing when you arrived," he said in a guarded voice, not like Galen at all. "We could have had a midnight supper for old times sake."

She shook her head as though he could see her. "I would have been no kind of company last night. I was cross-eyed with weariness. Will you be coming over?"

"I thought we could catch the outdoor concert tonight. Sound good?"

"Sounds great. I missed the concerts more than anything." She hesitated. She had understood from Mr. Harwood that Galen would have a day off when she arrived. Their relationship was no secret at the office. "Will you be here this afternoon?"

"It doesn't look like I can," came his reply. "In fact, you'd better drop by the office today, if you can. A briefing would be beneficial to you before the upcoming staff meeting."

With as much time as she spent on the phone and reading all the correspondence he had sent her way, she felt she was well-briefed now. Could it be that Galen's feelings were more hurt than she had realized? She had made the mistake of riding slipshod over Rayne; it wouldn't do to make the same mistake twice. Tact and courtesy, that's the ticket!

"Fine, Galen," she agreed. "Whatever you say. You know better than I what's going on over there. I'll get unpacked and be there by one-thirty. Okay?"

She sensed his tension easing somewhat. "Good. I'll see you then. And, welcome home."

It was with sheer delight that Alecia hung her clothes in her own closet once again. There, in the back of her closet, was her rose-colored suit—one of Galen's favorites. She had almost forgotten about it.

That afternoon she donned the suit and took special pains with her appearance before leaving for the office. She would be especially kind to Galen and try to help him understand why she was detained in Oklahoma and why she was unable to call him.

He was alone in his office when she arrived. His secretary greeted Alecia with an expression of disbelief. "You finally came back," she said. "It's so good to see you again. He's in there. Want me to hold calls?"

Alecia smiled and nodded before knocking at his door and letting herself in.

All the stiffness that Galen put forth over the phone disappeared as he looked up and saw her standing there. His boyish expression seemed older somehow, more intense.

"Alecia." He breathed out the word. "I've missed you." He lay down the pen in his hand, quietly rolled the chair back, and rose to step around the desk and take her in his arms.

After struggling and fighting her emotions with Rayne,

it was a relief to relax in Galen's arms and return his embrace and his warm kisses.

The following weeks were filled with hard work as she strove to put together the details and finishing touches on their project. There were artists, performers, and business people to contact, soliciting the services of ones who cared enough to become involved.

She and Galen worked closely together and his initial coldness faded as he became more enthusiastic than ever about their relationship. In their work each day, he went out of his way to be kind and understanding to her. Socially, they went out several evenings a week and to church together each Sunday. But it seemed to Alecia like a surface relationship. Galen was as gracious to her as she could ever hope a man to be. Why then was she floundering so? Why was she so unsettled in her feelings?

The evening of the Fourth of July, they attended a glorious fireworks display in the park near her apartment. Later, hand-in-hand, they walked through the fragrant flower beds, when Galen pulled her to a stop and invited her to sit with him on one of the benches. A hint of breeze gave a whisper in the leaves of the sprawling shade trees above them.

"Alecia," he began, taking her hand in his. "I want to talk with you about our future. Mr. Harwood has offered me a position in his immediate office. He says he likes the way I've been handling what we've been doing. It looks like I have a great future there." He pulled a small box from his pocket. "But no matter what the future holds, I want all of our tomorrows to be shared together. Will you marry me? I love you desperately."

Alecia was astonished at the size of the ring in the box. As a girl she had often dreamed of having a man present her with a ring like this. But storybook dreams have a way of being distorted in real life. Later, she wondered if he had expected her to come alive with a positive reaction. If so, it must have been awkward and painful for him when she sat there, quietly staring at the sparkling diamond, having no idea what to say.

Of course, she could marry Galen and possibly be happy the rest of her life. They had talked much about their mutual enjoyment of the arts, of children, of sports, and scores of other things.

"It's gorgeous," she said finally. "I'm flattered that it's being offered to me. But marriage is such an enormous step in life." Once again—for the umpteenth time—she asked herself if her appreciation of Galen constituted real love that would last a lifetime.

"I know what a big step it is. That's why I've waited until I was sure before asking you."

"I had no idea you'd purchased the ring. I'm tempted to receive it simply because it's so lovely. Please, though, be patient with me. Let me think it over."

Silently, he closed the lid of the velvet-lined box. The taciturn manner she had sensed when she had returned home in May, was surfacing again. "All right, Alecia. You think about it and let me know. I'm going to my brother's home in Duluth for a few days. I'm taking off work until next Wednesday. I'd thought about asking you to go since you love Jenny and the kids. But, perhaps this would be a good time to spend apart, thinking and praying about our decision."

Sweet Galen. Always so methodical and proper about everything. "That sounds like a good idea. When you come back, I'll have an answer for you." Strange, she thought, that he should want to take a few days off now,

but not when she came home. Such a piddling matter.
Why should it annoy her so? She must be growing
paranoid.

She received his gentle kiss at her door and they said
goodbye. As she let herself in, she almost wished he would
get really angry. At least she would know what he was
feeling.

On Saturday morning, she was up early. To her way of
thinking, the Minneapolis summer was too magnificent to
waste sleeping it away. The gardens around the lake were
breathtaking and she hit the jogging trail early each
morning, before the sun became too warm.

She pulled on her sweats and went to the kitchen to pour
a glass of juice. Sounds of movement came from Delia's
room. Luckily, both of them were early risers. However,
whereas Alecia was anxious to get outdoors, Delia was
anxious to get to her easel.

As almost a second thought, Alecia decided to quickly
shampoo her hair and let it dry as she jogged. Later, when
the doorbell rang, she knew from experience that Delia
would not answer it—the weekend artist never wanted to
stop once she was started. "Don't disturb me unless it's a
life or death matter," she would order firmly.

Piling a thick towel upon her wet head, Alecia was
tempted to take difference with her roommate at this point.
Delia may be busy creatively, but at least she was present-
able.

There was no one of Alecia's acquaintance who would
be up this early on Saturday. Unless Delia had a new
boyfriend she had been keeping under wraps. Maybe it
was a package, or a telegram. Her heart quickened. She
hoped it had nothing to do with her parents—or Nancy!

Approaching the door, she could hear muffled voices on

the other side.

As she opened it, a little voice called out, "Surprise!" And it definitely was!

eleven

Rayne was leaning against the wall, with his hat tipped cockily forward, and wearing a grin that rivaled the Cheshire cat's. Beside him, dressed in typical tourist fashion of pink shorts, shirt, and even pink Nikes with tennis socks, was Joanna—sans cast!

Alecia couldn't help but laugh at their expressions. No doubt they were laughing at hers. "I don't suppose you thought of calling ahead," she scolded, covering her shock.

Rayne shrugged. "You know how it is with kids and surprises."

"I ought to." They laughed again at their ridiculous hallway conversation. "Joanna, welcome to Minneapolis." She reached down to hug the girl. How she had missed her. "Come on in here," she ordered, ushering the two of them in. "How's the old head?" she wanted to know. "And the cast is off." Joanna's hair was a scant longer now. Quite attractive.

"My head's fine and the cast came off last week." She kicked the leg. "Feels so good to have it off." Her large eyes darted about the apartment, taking it all in. "Daddy and I are here on a business trip," she announced with aplomb.

"Oh, really?" Alecia looked at Rayne.

"The livestock show at the Convention Hall." His eyebrows went up. "Don't tell me you haven't heard?"

"You know how it is," she retorted. "Been so swamped

around here, I clean forgot to catch the farm and market report each morning."

He pressed his lips together and shook his head. "Unforgivable. Wait till Nancy hears how you've fallen away in the short time you've been gone."

Joanna looked up at them. "Why do you two always talk so silly?" she asked. And they laughed again over the nothingness of it all.

"Miss Winland," Joanna said, "we want you to come to the livestock show with us. We're showing some of our livestock. It's going to be fun. Can you come?"

Looking at Joanna's face, waves of memories rushed over Alecia of the hours the child lay so deathly still. Now, here she was, not only recovered, but free from the shackles of her father's former fears. It was like beholding a miracle.

"Do we have to decide now?" she asked. "Why don't you sit down for a moment and let me get you something to drink and we'll talk about it."

Agreeing, Joanna bounded into the living room and sat down on the couch. Rayne's presence seemed to shrink the apartment. He maneuvered his long legs between the couch and the coffee table.

Joanna might blend into the throngs of summer tourists but Rayne never would. His tall form dressed in the pale green western suit, commanded attention. The hat in his hands he placed on the table before him.

"I want you to meet my roommate," Alecia told them, hoping she could get Delia out long enough so she could slip away and dry her hair. "Delia!" she called out, knowing in advance what the answer would be.

"In a minute. Just a few more strokes on this scene."

"It's hard to interrupt genius," Alecia explained.

Joanna was studying her surroundings. "Is this where you live all the time?"

"All the time," Alecia confirmed.

"Is this all there is to it?"

"Well, no." Alecia realized how small it must look to her, although it was large compared to most city apartments. "Come up here and see the kitchen." She led her up the few steps to the small kitchen, which she felt was just the right size not to waste a step, as she and Delia fixed their meals, both large and small.

"Oh." Joanna was not too impressed.

"The bedrooms are in the back. Delia's is down that hall, and mine is down that hall."

Her brown eyes were still questioning. "Where's your yard and how do you get to it?"

"Come here," Alecia said, attempting to conceal her amusement. "I'll show you my yard." This little rancher was bewildered by life in a high-rise.

Alecia took her to the window of her bedroom that overlooked the lake and the expanse of gardens surrounding it. In the early morning sun, the entire park looked like a garden from a fairyland.

"Wow!" At last, Joanna began to show a spark of interest. "All that is yours?"

"Actually, it belongs to the city, but they let me use it every day. See that path down there? I was about to go jogging among the roses this morning before you arrived."

"It's so pretty." Her nose was flattened against the window. "I'd like to see the water up close."

Alecia led the way back to the kitchen and put on the coffee maker, wondering how this day was going to work out. Should she go with them? She had no interest in a livestock show for heaven's sake, but they had come all this way.

Delia finally emerged from her room, having washed most of the paint smudges from her hands and face. "Sorry I took so long, folks, but when an artist. . .hey! Don't tell me. This must be the little lady who lost the battle with the cow."

"Steer," Joanna corrected.

"Excuse me. Steer," Delia agreed with a chuckle. "And this must be her father, Rayne. I've heard about you two. Greetings and welcome to the Minnie-apple. The great metropolitan snowball. Good thing you came after the thaw. You'll love it here. . .now."

Rayne was openly amused at her fast talking and her nasal twang. He shook her hand and drawled his greeting back to her.

Quickly, Alecia set her roomie to pouring the coffee and fixing Joanna chocolate milk, while she excused herself to dry her hair. "Delia, tell them about the city and what to see. You've lived here longer than I have."

Before the droning of the hair dryer drowned out Delia's voice, Alecia heard her saying, "Livestock show? Sounds like fun! I bet Alecia would love to go."

Fun, my foot. Alecia fluffed furiously at her hair with her fingers. The only reason Delia would consider going to a livestock show would be to search for subjects for her paintings.

Her chestnut curls flew about her face, much too full for her liking. She preferred to dry it running in the sunshine, rather than using the blow dryer. And it seemed to have a mind of its own today. She applied a touch of quick makeup, then fastened her hair back with a silk ribbon.

When she returned to the living room, Delia was deep in detail with Joanna about the Children's Theatre Company and what was playing there presently. Joanna was enthralled—especially now that she had made her own debut on stage!

Rayne glanced up at Alecia. "That really was you under there, wasn't it?" he quipped. Then he stood. "Alecia, we've got to run. There are endless details to be taken care of at Convention Hall. We just wanted to come by and invite you to join us this afternoon. Can we pick you up at one o'clock?"

Her mind was made up. If they wanted her with them, then she wanted to go. "That's fine, Rayne, but let's do one better than that. Let Joanna stay with us. You take care of your business, then come back for both of us."

Joanna bubbled over at the suggestion. "Can I, Daddy? Please? Then I can go jogging in Miss Winland's backyard down there by the flowers and the water."

Rayne thought a minute, then gave a guilty smile. "It's still hard to let go. Sure, she can stay. I'll be back here at one o'clock, sharp. You two had better be ready," he warned with a broad smile.

After Rayne left, and Joanna finished her chocolate milk, then two of them took the elevator to the street and crossed the busy thoroughfare to the park. "Is that ankle strong enough for jogging?" Alecia asked as they reached the path.

"Doctor said to exercise it as much as I could," she answered.

"Good." But Alecia slowed her pace anyway. "I didn't know ranchers took vacations," she commented as they progressed through the first leg of the jogging trail. "What made your daddy decide to bring exhibits to the livestock show?"

"It's not a real vacation," Joanna explained.

"But you are away from the ranching operations."

"Daddy's different now," she said simply. "One day he said, 'Joanna, we're going to travel more. You need to see something other than Oklahoma.' " Joanna had stopped to watch two swans glide delicately across the lake, leaving a silent riffle behind them. Alecia stood beside her.

"He's happy more of the time now, too," the girl continued. "He never gets real mad like he used to." She dug the toe of her Nike into the grass. "If it took being thrown and gored by a longhorn to change him, Miss Winland, then I'm glad I got hurt," she concluded with childlike sincerity.

"Those are strong words. But I think I know what you mean. It shouldn't take calamities to wake us adults up, but sometimes it does. We can be pretty hard-headed, you know."

Joanna laughed. "Yeah, I know. Like Uncle Lavren."

Alecia involuntarily shivered at sound of the name. "What about him?"

"He's gone to Hawaii."

"Hawaii? What in the world is he doing in Hawaii?"

"Aunt Corrine went, too. She says it's like their second honeymoon. She's says he's nicer now."

"Is that right?"

Joanna nodded. "Know what Daddy says?"

"Tell me quick. What does Daddy say?"

"Daddy says there's been more than one miracle in Denlin County since you came there."

Alecia felt herself blushing and hoped the redness from exertion disguised it. But as usual, Joanna was unaffected. Looking around her as they jogged on, she said, "This is an awful pretty place. I can see why you wanted to come back, but I'm homesick already. I miss my horse."

Now it was Alecia's turn to laugh. "Well, ignore those feelings and come on. When we finish the course, I'll show you a cute dress shop in the mall down the street."

"Miss Winland, I've been thinking." Joanna changed her jogging to happy little skips. "Since you're not my teacher now, can I call you Alecia? Like a friend?"

Alecia thought about it briefly. "I guess that would be permissible."

"Oh, goody, goody." The skips changed to little rabbit hops as they wound around to the end of the trail.

They were ready at one o'clock sharp just as Rayne instructed. Alecia changed into a comfortable skirt and blouse and sturdy walking shoes. She knew the size of the Convention Hall.

Delia waited until Rayne arrived before revealing her little tidbit of news. Alecia thought surely her roommate was above conniving little schemes. But she was wrong. With a sly smile, Delia asked Joanna, "How would you like to go with me to the Children's Theatre tonight? I just found out where I can get two tickets for great seats."

The brown eyes came alive. "The theatre like you were telling me about? Wow! Would I? But I don't know if I can. Can I, Daddy?" She looked up at Rayne.

"That's real nice of you, Delia," Rayne began, "but you didn't have to go to the trouble."

"Trouble? Ask Alecia here. I'm always looking for excuses to go to Children's Theatre. Looks kind of silly for a grown woman to go all by herself. You know?"

Alecia nodded with a little chuckle. It was so true. Her kooky friend loved that theatre more than all the others.

"Well," he intoned thoughtfully. "If you're sure."

"I'm sure. I'm sure. Meanwhile, Alecia can show you

how downtown Minneapolis glows at night. I bet she's been dying to get you into a Greek or French restaurant."

Alecia loved her companion's complete lack of subtlety. "I would at that," she agreed. So within minutes, the day was planned and it looked great.

Several of Rayne's men had driven up earlier in the week, bringing not only the cattle, but a few of the horses as well. Sammy, of course, stayed behind to run the ranch.

The livestock show was unlike anything Alecia had ever seen. A spectacular showing of the prime of America's cattle, horses, hogs, and sheep. She was amazed at the magnitude of it all. Together, they strolled through endless rows of stalls filled with every type and breed of livestock. At one point, Joanna gave an excited shout. "There's our stall. That's our cattle."

Over the stalls hung bright royal blue banners with EL CROSSE emblazoned in white. Rayne explained to Alecia that he hadn't bothered with shows for the past few years, even though he was confident he had prize-winning stock, and was well aware that winning shows helped to advertise breeding stock. But up until now, he said, it had seemed to be too much trouble.

Alecia knew this reluctance was due to his desire to withdraw from any outside activities that attracted attention to himself or to Joanna.

They continued viewing exhibits and Alecia found her interest growing as Rayne outlined the details of competition to her. The animal aromas, mixed with that of hay and leather, brought back memories of her work for Nancy and the thought of the quiet tranquility that was ever-present there.

The equine exhibits were the grandest of all, and Alecia

hoped she could attend a day of judging next week. The competition would be exciting to watch.

"Now you get to see Midnight Melody," Joanna told her. "I've always wanted you to see her."

"Midnight Melody? Who is she?" Alecia was being pulled along quickly by Joanna's tugging at her arm.

"Daddy's best horse. She's beautiful. She'll take home the prizes. Wait and see."

They led her to yet another stall proudly displaying the El Crosse banner on the cross bar. And there she was! A horse every bit as beautiful as Corrine's, and more so. Midnight's coat was a deep sorrel that shaded into an ebony mane, tail, and legs. She was simply magnificent.

Alecia gasped. "She's so lovely." How thrilling it would be to work with a horse like this. Secretly, Alecia had decided to locate a stable in the city and enroll in riding lessons. She had so much to learn. Aloud, she mused, "Twilight Song and Midnight Melody. . .similar names. Any connection?"

"From the same dam," Rayne told her. "Both winners, but I haven't pressed to show. I don't want to step on Corrine's toes. I'll try showing where she isn't in competition."

Alecia laughed at that. "Quite considerate of you, but I'm sure Corrine can handle herself—win or lose."

"She can at that," he replied with a slight smile.

He moved into the stall to check to see that all was as it should be, talking easily to the filly as he worked.

"My horse, Kaney-Kins is a winner, too," Joanna was saying. "Daddy's given me permission to start practicing my barrel racing. Next fall I might be ready for the Denlin County Rodeo."

"Kaney-Kins?" Alecia repeated. "Don't tell me. Related to Nancy's horses?" Nancy had never told her.

"Raisin Kane is the sire of Joanna's filly," Rayne said from inside the stall as he bent to check Midnight's feet. "By the way, Nancy said to tell you Kane Brake will foal in the fall."

"How delightful." Alecia's head swam with all these fascinating names and wonderful mounts. Of course, she knew it wasn't all fame and glory, for she had tasted of the hard work involved. She knew the price that was paid.

Rayne's ranch hands, Josh and Brock, came by and Alecia was introduced to them. They remembered her as the schoolteacher who couldn't get her car started at the ranch one day. She strove not to blush, and Rayne grinned at her.

When it was time to go, Alecia found she wasn't ready to leave the grandeur of it all. But they needed time to get ready for their evening out.

In front of her high-rise, Alecia stepped to the curb from the taxi, and Rayne stepped out with her. "I'll see you in a couple of hours." He paused as though there was something else on his mind. He stammered a moment then said, "Are you sure this is all right. . .this thing with Delia and Joanna?"

Alecia gave him a patient smile. Remnants of the over-protective, widowed father. "It's more than all right," she assured him. "They'll have the time of their lives. Delia's a nut and she loves kids." In a teasing tone, she added, "Uh, are you sure it's all right. . .this thing with Rayne and Alecia?"

He shot her a sheepish grin and pushed back his hat. "Touché, my friend. I'll see you later." He folded himself back into the cab and father and daughter waved as they drove away.

If she had been apprehensive before, she was more so when she learned Galen had called while she was out. "What did you tell him?" she quizzed Delia.

"I told him you had unexpected guests from Oklahoma drop in."

"Is that all?"

Delia snickered. "I didn't tell him the most handsome rancher ever to stomp a boot stepped into our apartment this morning. But I could have. . .and not exaggerated."

"Delia, have mercy. Am I supposed to call him back?"

"Yes ma'am. As soon as possible."

Hurriedly, she dialed Galen's brother's number in Duluth. Galen's voice was pleasant as ever as he greeted her. "Alecia. So good to hear your voice. I feel I've been gone a week rather than just a day. I want you to know that although you caused me a little confusion, I'm not angry with you. Please understand that."

"I understand, Galen. Likewise, you'll have to understand my position and my feelings."

"I love you, Alecia, and I want you to be my wife, but I'll be as patient as I can. I guess it's just that I hoped it wouldn't have to be something you'd have to think over."

"Marriage is sacred to me. It'll have to be 'till death do us part' in my life."

"You know we agree on that."

She did know. They agreed on so many things. What then was her holdup? Why was she torturing him like this? But that inexplicable, nameless restlessness could not be ignored.

"I'm glad you have company," he went on. "Friends of your sister's?"

Alecia forced herself to be honest. "It's the little girl

who was in the hospital. . .she and her father are here."

"I see." Galen changed the subject then and began describing the delightful antics of his charming nieces who were ages two and four. They laughed together, although to Alecia the laughter seemed stiff and empty.

When she hung up and came into the kitchen for a cup of coffee, Delia took a look at her and gave a low whistle. "You two have a fight?"

"No. Why?"

"The long face."

"Actually, I haven't told you this, but Galen offered me a ring the night of the Fourth."

"Oooh, honey. What did you say? Obviously, you turned him down."

"I told him I needed time to think and pray about it."

"Are you praying?"

Alecia nodded, sipping at the hot coffee, not really wanting to drink it. She poured it to occupy her hands while her mind was spinning. "I am. But I'm still so confused. He's a wonderful guy. So diligent in his work, and kind and considerate."

Delia's eyes twinkled. "Rayne's a wonderful guy!"

"Delia! Be serious. Rayne has nothing to do with this."

Delia plopped down on the couch and put her feet up. "Oh really? If a good looking guy like that came all the way from Oklahoma to see me, I wouldn't be taking it as lightly as you are."

"Hey, you're supposed to be the level-headed one in this group. Is this why you've manipulated this evening so Rayne and I could be alone tonight? Rayne came up here for a livestock show. A place to show his livestock." She enunciated the words like a grammar teacher.

"Sure, sure. Now you're going to tell me this show—

taking place in the city where you just happen to live—was the only one available in the nation. Right? Wow, are you dense."

Delia was speaking forth things she had been frightened to say even silently to herself. She shook her head. "I don't know. I think he's just overly grateful. Plus Joanna's crazy about me. That's all."

"Okay, have it your way." Delia hopped up to go get ready. "But if I were you, I'd wake up and be sure."

In the quiet of her room, Alecia changed into her white eyelet sundress with the delicate pink ribbon-and-lace trim. In her mind, she fought against the things about which Delia hinted. Was there a chance that Rayne might actually love her?

She remembered the evening of the party at Corrine's. Had he sought her out because he truly cared for her, in spite of their harsh differences at the time? And was that why he had picked this show to attend...to once again seek her out? To be with her?

The thoughts bewildered her. Whatever would she say if he expressed his love to her? Did she love him in return? Or was it simply infatuation?

She vigorously brushed back her hair and fastened each side with pink satin ribbons, then fluffed the bangs across her forehead.

She was sure there could never be a life for her with Rayne. Even the very notion was ridiculous. Her a rancher's wife? Impossible. And besides, she told herself once again, his attachment to her was merely one of gratification. Her mother always told her once you showed someone God's mercy, that person would be forever indebted to you. And that was enough, really. To know that Rayne now trusted God and was taking Joanna to church regularly.

In times past, she recklessly let her emotions fly out of hand. She was determined not to allow that to happen again. Granted, she was flattered Rayne wanted to spend time with her, but she would remain level-headed about the entire situation.

From her bedside table, she took her soft, worn Bible and turned again to Philippians 4:11, the verse she continually prayed would be fulfilled in her life. "For I have learned, in whatsoever state I am, therewith to be content," she softly murmured.

"Well, I'm learning," she told herself. She could be content that Rayne wanted to be friends. That was good enough. Plus she was thrilled to once again see Joanna. At least there was one area where she had no confusion. She deeply loved that little girl.

Showing Rayne the city was great fun. They meandered through Nicollet Mall and ate fresh fruit in a skyway café. They took in a play that turned out to be uproariously funny and they enjoyed much-needed hearty laughs together.

Later, they viewed the city from the observation deck atop the IDS building. As Rayne beheld the metroplex with its relentless, steady streams of moving traffic and wildly flashing lights, he pushed back his hat with his thumb and shook his head slowly. "Don't you ever feel bunched up and hemmed in with all these people? It's enough to strangle a guy."

Alecia looked at the same scene with eyes that perceived the excitement and promise that it held. "Well," she admitted, "at one time, I was unaware of the peace and tranquility of the wide open spaces. I'd never experienced the feeling of being at one with God while looking out across an open plain and watching Him paint a new, fresh sunset each evening."

"And now?"

"Now that I've tasted of that. . .being very close to nature. . .yes, I must confess, since I've come back, I do feel a trifle hemmed in at times."

He nodded.

She hastened to add, "Actually, it's like taking a vacation to the Bahamas and enjoying the beauty and climate. Naturally, a person misses that when he returns to his own work-a-day world, but it doesn't override the love for home. I also see the beauty and excitement here."

Still, she could tell by his face that he thought it incredible that anyone could live in such a hectic, crowded place.

Leaving the tower, he said, "We were going to eat sometime tonight, weren't we? Where are those foreign places Delia talked about? I'm so hungry I could eat a bobcat."

Alecia laughed. "No place that I know carries that item on the menu. Is it some sort of local native delicacy in the lowlands of Oklahoma?"

They caught a cab to a dimly lit French place at Saint Anthony Main. Rayne wasn't deterred by the strange cuisine nor the menu, but continued to pelt the patient waiter with questions until he was clear on every item.

Alecia was well-acquainted with the menu, but remained silent and let him fare for himself. He did remarkably well. Secretly, she thought he would be like a fish out of water, but instead she was admiring him for adjusting so smoothly.

They lingered over their meal in the restful surroundings, engaged in relaxed conversation that seemed to flow easily. Lapses in their talk didn't scream out for forced remarks. If ever Alecia longed for a moment of time to be endless, this was surely that moment. Although she had been here dozens of times, she had never been so intoxicated with the atmosphere. Had Rayne made that much difference in her life?

Rayne's broad hand covered her smaller one. His infectious smile was brighter than ever. Leaning forward, he asked, "Has anyone ever told you that you're very beautiful?"

"Yes," she replied, surprised she could remain so casual, so relaxed. "Several have."

"Well then. . .," the smile widened. "Has anyone ever told you your hair has a glossy sheen as lovely as a sorrel filly's?"

Her soft laughter spilled out into the golden glow between them. "I can honestly tell you, Mr. Lassiter, that no one ever has."

"Good," he said, lifting her hand and planting kisses on each fingertip. "I selfishly wanted to be the first one."

With a warm inner knowing, Alecia realized if she never saw Rayne again the rest of her life, this delightful portion of merriment and close companionship shared this special evening, could never be taken from her.

Rayne's muscular arm held her close on the way to her apartment. Just before the cab came to a stop, he touched her cheek to turn her face to his to kiss her. "Thank you for a marvelous evening," he whispered.

The restrained, gentle kiss held none of the abandoned release of emotions as that rainy day in the stable. Yet, the same thundering explosions were going off inside Alecia. Desperately, she clutched her emotions to her heart and held them there in silence.

They found Delia and Joanna having a giggling good

time over popcorn and a game of Scrabble. Rayne's
pleased expression told Alecia it was yet another new step
for him to see Joanna getting on so famously with a virtual
stranger.

Sunday held special moments as they worshipped together at Alecia's church. Waves of joy swept over her
and they stood to sing the melodious hymns—she and
Rayne with Joanna between them. At odd moments they
caught glances and smiled at one another. Rayne's sono-
rous baritone voice was full and rich. At the closing
prayer, Joanna surprised them by taking each of their
hands and placing them together on her lap.

After lunch in the mall, Rayne asked Alecia, "Do you
remember that long ago you promised to play me a game
of tennis?"

She felt herself go crimson as she recalled where they
were when he commented on the strength in her arms. "I
vaguely remember it being mentioned."

"Good. Then let's use this sunny afternoon for you to
show your stuff on the courts."

"Tell me," she retorted, "did you bring your tennis
boots?"

It turned out to be another time of carefree hilarity.
Never had she laughed so much, nor been challenged so
strongly in her game. She got the last one over on him, but
he had already won two.

"Oh, well," she sighed and rubbed the back of her neck
with her towel. "It was worth it just to see the Oklahoma
rancher in tennis togs."

He snapped her on the leg with the tip of his towel.

Never had she known such joy in being with a person.
But she was confident it was because she had made the
decision not to become emotionally involved, but to

simply enjoy Rayne as a friend.

There was more business for Rayne to attend to Sunday evening at Convention Hall. They parted after their tennis match with the promise that she would be at the Convention Hall Tuesday evening as soon as she got off work. She found herself counting the minutes.

She took her jump suit to work with her Tuesday to change into, and was more than anxious to get over to the Convention Hall that evening to see what was going on. As agreed, they met at Midnight's stall, then ate supper together at one of the snack bars.

"A far cry from the little French café," Rayne said as they quickly downed the tasteless hamburgers. But he had much to do to get ready.

Before judging time, Joanna and Alecia went to the stands and Joanna filled her in on what the judges were looking for. The competition was a long drawn-out, but exciting, affair. Had it not been for Joanna's explanations, the judging would have made little sense to Alecia.

The arena was filled with well-groomed horses in their best form, performing flawlessly for their trainers. Rayne had changed into a golden tan suit with matching hat, and Midnight Melody wore a stunning silver saddle and bridle.

It wasn't until Midnight Melody's name came blaring over the loudspeaker as the grand champion winner, that Alecia realized how tense she had been. Suddenly, she and Joanna were hugging one another, and cheering, and laughing.

There was a time of congratulating, photo taking, and awarding of the trophies that accompanied being a winner. Alecia watched, entranced, from the sidelines.

When Rayne was finally free, he hugged her openly. "We did it!" he exclaimed. "We won it!" He released

Alecia and swept Joanna giggling off her feet and swung her around. "Let's celebrate. Where would you like to go?"

"You look a little tired," Alecia told him. "Let's just call Delia to have something ready at my apartment."

He rubbed at his mustache and grinned. "You're right, smart teacher lady. I'm bushed. I'll take care of Midnight and we'll go."

By the time they arrived, Delia had ordered two large pizzas and had soft drinks chilled. They couldn't have had a grander celebration at the most exquisite eating place in town. With Rayne, a person could have fun anywhere.

They were laughing about the spewing soda pop when the doorbell rang and Delia went to answer it.

Alecia looked up from where she and Rayne were standing near the kitchen to see Galen enter the living room.

twelve

"Galen." Alecia stepped toward him.

"I came back early," he said flatly, his face expressionless. "Thought I would drop by and meet your guests."

Distressed, Alecia made the introductions between Rayne and Joanna and Galen.

Rayne was kind. "I've heard lots of good things about you from Alecia," he remarked, although she had hardly mentioned Galen's name.

"Won't you have something, Galen?" Delia waved her hand toward the last of the pizza. "We were celebrating the Lassiters' win at the livestock show."

"Really? No, I've got to be going, thank you. I didn't mean to intrude." His attitude was saddening and exasperating.

Alecia wished she knew what to say. How could she ever explain? She knew how Rayne must look to him. She would have to try to clear it up later.

In a moment, he had excused himself and was gone. It seemed to put a damper on the gaiety.

"I hope I didn't cause any problems," Rayne told her later when Joanna was in Delia's studio looking at the paintings.

"No, no. Don't be silly. Things aren't that serious between us."

"He looked crushed."

"Yes, he did. But that's not your fault."

"I didn't intend to come here and mess up your life."

175

She looked at his gentle face. "You could never do that."

"Alecia." He sat down beside her on the couch. "We'll be flying out of here in the morning. I want to thank you for a wonderful time. I don't know when I've ever had so much plain old fun."

"It has been fun, Rayne. It's a treat to be friends with someone like you."

She thought he was going to say something further, but at that moment, Joanna came bounding out, insisting he come and see Delia's great paintings.

The evening was over too soon and a strange quiet settled into Alecia's heart and mind.

The next morning, before Rayne and Joanna caught their plane, they called Alecia at the office and said their last goodbyes over the phone. "I wish you great success in your work," Rayne told her. She had explained to him that Galen was being moved up and she was soon to move into his office. It was a real step up for her. One she had been waiting for.

"Thank you, Rayne. I wish you the same."

"I'll miss you, Alecia," Joanna was saying with tears in her voice. "I wish we didn't live so far away from each other."

"Me, too, honey. Me, too."

And then they were gone. It had been difficult to get over being away from Joanna last May. Now she found it doubly hard—for she knew she missed Rayne as well.

She tried, however feebly, to break the news to Galen that she could not marry him. She was certain of it now. When she married, it would be to someone like Rayne Lassiter. Of that she was certain.

Poor Galen could not separate in his mind the fact that she said no and the fact that he saw her having fun with

Rayne in the apartment that evening. She assured him that Rayne had nothing to do with her decision. But, in a way he did. Oh, it was all so impossible to sort out in her mind. How could she ever help him to see, when she didn't understand it herself?

After that, Galen seldom called, and later his promotion put him in another area of the office building. Her days grew somewhat lonely. In the evenings, she spent her spare time at a riding stable. She drove out once a week for her lessons, and other times simply to ride. She had fallen hopelessly in love with horses.

She and the stable owner often discussed just which horse would be right for her to own. Her deepest desire was to purchase a colt and train it. But what did she know about training horses?

She dated a few men from her office, but none were the type of person she enjoyed being with, so that halted.

Notes arrived from Joanna. They were attending more shows and still winning. Her neat little handwriting said she had entered her first rodeo and won third place in her age division in barrel racing. Rayne never wrote, but Joanna always ended her letter, "Daddy says 'hi.' " Likewise, Alecia ended hers to Joanna, "Tell your daddy 'hi' for me."

There were activities at church in which she and Delia were involved that were both entertaining and fun. But her inner restlessness clung like a cocklebur in Peppy's mane.

She assumed that when school began, and she could see her project put into operation, the annoying sensation would be quenched. So, when September rolled around and her jogging times were chilly from a distinct fall nip in the air, she was disturbed that the hollow nameless thing was still attached to her.

"What, Lord?" she would ask Him as she trotted around the paths and surveyed the crimson and gold trees. "What are You trying to tell me? What am I not hearing? I'm doing everything within my power to serve You and live for You. What is this awful void in me?"

She was almost jealous of her parents as she read their letters from South America. Walt and Mattie were having such a gratifying time serving the Lord together. One Sunday at church, Alecia lingered behind after the service to talk to her pastor about filling out applications for missions. After all, she was a trained educator. Surely, she would be needed.

But that evening as she looked them over, Delia gave her a knowing grin and said, "Mmm. Most missionaries I know apply because God calls them, not because they are at loose ends."

Alecia wadded up the forms and hook-shot them into the waste basket.

The call that settled the issue came in the wee hours of the morning. She nearly knocked the phone off the bedside table as she grabbed for it, and struggled to awaken herself.

"Miss Winland, please."

"Speaking."

"Ma'am, this is Dr. Islip, Denlin County Hospital. Your sister had a light stroke and was brought in by a neighbor, Mr. Shanks, earlier in the evening."

Alecia sat straight up in her bed, swinging her feet to the floor. "Nancy? Oh, no!" Her heart pressed into her throat like a cold, hard stone. "How is she now?" Please, Lord, let me think clearly.

"She's holding steady at present. Thankfully, she was discovered by her neighbor who then called the ambulance."

Good old Jake, she thought warmly. He had watched out for Nancy after all.

"You stayed with Mrs. Whitlow after her surgery last winter didn't you? I believe I remember you."

"Yes, I was there."

"Do any members of your family live closer to Oklahoma?"

"No," she said, "I'm the nearest one."

"Then I suggest you come as soon as you can."

Alecia shivered in the early morning chill, tucked the phone under her chin, and grabbed for her robe. "I'll catch the first flight out, Dr. Islip. Please tell Jake to meet me at the airport."

"Certainly."

Immediately, she roused Delia and together they prayed for the day that lay ahead for Alecia. By nine that morning, she was gazing down at the clouds beneath her plane, wondering how her new assistant could possibly handle the details of the project while she was gone.

Her initial fright had waned and she was sure that Nancy, the fighter, would come through like a winner. A stroke was more serious than major surgery, but Nancy would make it.

And this would be a short stay this time, she reasoned. She couldn't get tangled into staying indefinitely as she had last spring. She would have to hire someone to stay with Nancy—perhaps a trained nurse. Or possibly their parents could come home for a furlough. Surely, the people of South America weren't more important than their own daughter.

Abruptly, Alecia stopped and shook her head as if to shake away the cobwebs of selfish reasoning. "Forgive me, Lord," she breathed as she viewed the glowing floor of clouds beneath them. "I want to learn to do Your will in this. Show me what to do."

A very somber Jake met her plane. As he drove her to the ranch in his ancient pickup, he described the frightening moment when he had returned to the house for no other reason but that he felt he should check on her one more time. He found her on the floor, struggling to crawl to the phone. "If I'd been plastered like I used to be all the time, I never would have found her," he said in a quavery voice.

"We're so grateful to you, Jake," she said gently. "So very grateful."

Nancy was no better, but only slightly coherent. There was great difficulty in understanding her. Her movements were stilted. Alecia was distressed to see her precious, loving sister suffering like this. Why had this happened to her? Someone so kind and good...always loving...always giving.

Rayne and Joanna were in Phoenix for a horse show, but when they returned and learned what had happened they were at the ranch to help.

Nancy resorted to writing out little notes of instructions with her left hand. Much work was yet to be done to get the place ready for winter.

The familiarity of the ranch was comforting. Dependable Peppy; excitable, hard-working Sparkie; proud Raisin Kane; and the very pregnant Kane Brake with her bulging sides—they all helped to make Alecia feel welcome.

It was difficult to explain later how it happened, but every evening Rayne was there—sometimes Jake, sometimes Joanna, but always Rayne. There wasn't time to talk about it, think about it, or ask questions. Only work to do between hospital visitations each day.

On the note pad, Nancy feebly scratched out, "Watch Kane Brake."

Alecia complied gladly. She was terribly excited about the prospect of the new foal.

The days were Indian summer—warm, fragrant, and golden. The hints and whiffs of lingering summer played teasingly with the signs of fall. The leaves on the oaks in Nancy's back yard began to fall ever so slowly onto the lawn that was still green. To crunch them underfoot was to release their pungent odors of autumn. Fall in Minneapolis was sometimes depressing to her, but here at the ranch, it felt pregnant with promise. She was so sure everything was going to be all right.

Together, she and Rayne rode the pastures and brought in the calves that Nancy wanted readied for the sale. The ones she didn't want to winter over. They checked fences and worked to be sure each feeder station was in good condition for the cold days to come. Alecia was more than thankful for her riding lessons. She was able to be of more help than before. Rayne commented on her improvement, which pleased her.

She wasn't as good a cook as Nancy, but with a freezer full of steaks, roasts, and ground beef, it wasn't too difficult to turn something out when Rayne and Jake were there late. There was still a gold mine of tomatoes, squash, and carrots in the waning garden. These Alecia reaped and added to the meals.

In the evenings, she and Rayne sat on the back patio with cups of coffee, taking in each golden splendorous sunset, breathing deeply of the clean, tangy fall air. Sometimes talking about the work, sometimes sitting in comfortable silence just thinking.

Each night Alecia fell into bed with a tiredness that was far removed from frustration. It was a genuine physical exhaustion that was erased with the dawn. Sleep was deep and restful.

Nancy improved slowly, steadily. Each afternoon, Alecia drove to the hospital to spend time by her sister's bedside—praying, talking, encouraging, reading Bible passages that Nancy requested to hear.

Calls to Minneapolis revealed that her assistant was doing well in her sink-or-swim position. Mr. Harwood told Alecia it was because of the excellent groundwork that she and Galen had laid out during the previous year that others were able to step in and carry on.

One evening after Jake left, Rayne went out to the stable for one more check on Kane Brake before leaving for home.

Alecia was finishing up in the kitchen. She had swept her hair up of off her neck in a casual do. It was an unusually warm October day. Presently, Rayne was calling to her from the back door. "Come quick! Kane Brake's about to foal!"

She dropped the things in her hands and rushed to his side, as full of excitement as a small child at Christmas.

Anxiously, the mare paced in her stall. At intervals she lay down for a few minutes, then arose and began pacing once again.

Alecia watched as Rayne worked with her. He had that special touch with animals. He spoke repeatedly to her in gentle tones to calm her. When she lay down again, and nickered and quivered in her frustration, Rayne was there at her head, talking. . .comforting.

A few hours passed slowly as they kept their vigil. Periodically, the mare would lie down and bear down with all her might, but the foal did not emerge.

"Looks like she may have a difficult time." His voice was tinged with worry.

"Oh, no. I hope not." Alecia bit her lip. "Nancy would be so disappointed if anything happened to this foal. She asks about him every day. She's counting on this little fellow."

Kane Brake nickered again plaintively and nipped at her flanks. She emitted pitiful moans to express the pains that the pressure of birthing were causing within her huge midsection.

Reluctantly, Alecia went inside to bring out coffee. As she busied herself, she began to pray for the safe birth of the colt. Somehow, it seemed to stand for something. For hope. . .for a new beginning.

When she returned, Rayne had donned rubber gloves from the vet bag in Nancy's tack room. "I was able to turn the foal," he explained. "One leg was twisted all out of position." He sighed, giving a weak smile as he removed the gloves. "I think it's okay now."

She left the stable door open. The night was clear and still. . .warm as summer. Carefully, she set down the tray with the coffee.

"Come quick, Alecia," Rayne called.

Just as she stepped to the stall, the foal began to emerge. In a fraction of a second, the miracle of birth was complete and the tiny creature was lying in a wet heap on the dropcloth that Rayne had carefully spread out.

"She's a filly," Rayne said excitedly.

Alecia was breathless with wonder and awe. She moved behind where he was kneeling and placed her hands on his shoulders to get a closer look. "A miracle of new life," she whispered.

Rayne lay his cheek over against her hand. "She's a miracle all right. She just about didn't make it."

The filly was sleek and wet with fluid, but immediately lifted her little head to sniff the air and greet the world. Kane Brake was busy cleaning her.

"Nancy told me I could name her," Alecia told him. "What do you think of Kandy Kane?"

He looked up at her. "That's a happy name. Sounds like something you would think of."

By now, Kandy was struggling to steady her forelegs and pull her hindquarters up under her body to stand. She was beautiful. Every part of her was perfect. In a matter of minutes, the quiet of the stable was filled with greedy, sucking sounds.

"Let's call Nancy," Alecia suggested.

"You go on in," Rayne told her. "I'll clean up around here and wash up. Then I'll be in."

Later, when Rayne stepped into Nancy's den, Alecia was sitting motionless in the wing-backed chair.

"Alecia." His voice was husky. "What's the matter?"

She forced her eyes to focus on his face. . .his kind, wonderful, concerned face. But the tears were hot and fiery in her eyes, blurring everything. . .blinding her. "She's gone, Rayne. Nancy's gone. They called me just now. . .before I could call her. Peacefully, in her sleep, only moments ago. On her note pad was one last note: 'The foal is Alecia's.'"

Rayne reached out to lift her to him and quietly gathered her into his broad chest. The tears flowed freely and the sobs shook her body.

"Oh, Rayne," she said, "I never got to tell her. Now she'll never know."

"What, Alecia? Tell me."

"It was so important for me to tell her." She drew away from his arms to stand by the glass-fronted stove that had no need yet of a warming fire. "I've been so confused lately. Restless and empty. But tonight as the foal was born, there came a new revelation sweeping over me. I knew in my heart this is where I belong." Another sob sent a shudder through her. "As I watched the exquisite miracle of birth, I felt like I'd come home. I...I can hardly express it. I just knew."

"Alecia, my precious darling," Rayne said to her. "How I've hoped and prayed to hear you say those words. That you would come to know beyond the shadow of a doubt, that this is the life you've chosen. Because I love you and I want you to share your life with me as my wife. The mistress of El Crosse, Joanna's mother, my friend, my lover."

Alecia dabbed at her tears with the handkerchief he pressed into her palm. Hearing him profess his love to her was like a dream come true. "Rayne, I love you, too. More than I ever hoped to love any man. But why didn't you tell me? I never dared to hope. . . ."

"I was unsure at first, and scared. It was all so crazy how I wanted to be with you, to hold you and keep you, and yet hating everything you were saying. Then, when I did know for sure, I thought perhaps you couldn't be happy being a rancher's wife." Gently, he kissed the top of her head as he held her shoulders.

"I talked to Nancy about it," he went on. "She told me to be patient and to keep praying. So I did. And here you are by my side."

She rested her face against his chest. "Nancy said she prayed that my experiences here would benefit me for a lifetime. Her prayers were full of effective power. I believe it's because of her prayers that we're here together right now."

Rayne lifted her face to gaze at her. "She knows, Alecia. I'm convinced, she knows." As he kissed her with the full unrestrained emotions of a man excited for his beloved to be his own, Alecia's head swam with the bittersweet emotions of losing Nancy, yet at the same moment finding her kind, gentle Rayne. He emitted to her his tender strength, and she was gladly strengthened by it.

"We'll check on little Kandy Kane," he whispered, "then I'll drive you to the hospital."

Arm-in-arm, they stepped out across the lawn to the stable. In the milky white light of a fat, swollen harvest moon, the fields lay peaceful and sleeping. They were her fields now. She had learned to be content. She had found her fields of sweet content.

A Letter To Our Readers

Dear Reader:

In order that we might better contribute to your reading enjoyment, we would appreciate your taking a few minutes to respond to the following questions. When completed, please return to the following:

Karen Carroll, Editor
Heartsong Presents
P.O. Box 719
Uhrichsville, Ohio 44683

1. Did you enjoy reading *Fields of Sweet Content*?
   ☐ Very much. I would like to see more books
      by this author!
   ☐ Moderately
      I would have enjoyed it more if _____

   _____

2. Are you a member of *Heartsong Presents*? Yes   No
   If no, where did you purchase this book? _____

   _____

3. What influenced your decision to purchase
   this book? (Circle those that apply.)

Cover	Back cover copy
Title	Friends
Publicity	Other _____

4. On a scale from 1 (poor) to 10 (superior), please rate the following elements.

___Heroine   ___Plot

___Hero   ___Inspirational theme

___Setting   ___Secondary characters

5. What settings would you like to see covered in *Heartsong Presents* books?

_____

_____

6. What are some inspirational themes you would like to see treated in future books?_____

_____

_____

7. Would you be interested in reading other *Heartsong Presents* titles?   Yes   No

8. Please circle your age range:
   Under 18   18-24   25-34
   35-45   46-55   Over 55

9. How many hours per week do you read? _____

Name _____

Occupation _____

Address _____

City _____ State _____ Zip _____

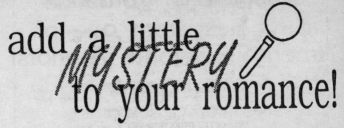
add *a little* MYSTERY to your romance!

TWO GREAT INSPIRATIONAL ROMANCES WITH JUST A TOUCH OF MYSTERY
BY MARLENE J. CHASE

_____*The Other Side of Silence*—Anna Durham finds a purpose for living in the eyes of a needy child and a reason to love in the eyes of a lonely physician...but first the silence of secrets must be broken. HP6 BHSB-07 $2.95.

_____*This Trembling Cup*— A respite on a plush Wisconsin resort may just be the thing for Angie Carlson's burn-out—or just the beginning of a devious plot unraveling and the promise of love. HP5 BHSB-05 $2.95.

Inspirational Romance
at its Best from one of
America's Favorite Authors!

FOUR HISTORICAL ROMANCES
BY COLLEEN L. REECE

___ *A Torch for Trinity*—When Trinity Mason sacrifices her teaching ambitions for a one-room school, her life—and Will Thatcher's—will never be the same. HP1 BHSB-01 $2.95

___*Candleshine*-A sequel to *A Torch for Trinity*—With the onslaught of World War II, Candleshine Thatcher dedicates her life to nursing, and then her heart to a brave Marine lieutenant. HP7 BHSB-06 $2.95

___*Wildflower Harvest*—Ivy Ann and Laurel were often mistaken for each other...was it too late to tell one man the truth? HP2 BHSB-02 $2.95

___ *Desert Rose*-A sequel to *Wildflower Harvest*—When Rose Birchfield falls in love with one of Michael's letters, and then with a cowboy named Mike, no one is more confused than Rose herself. HP8 BHSB-08 $2.95